# ANGELS IN ALASKA-tm

### ANGEL'S DIAMONDS

### ANGEL'S TREASURE

### ANGEL'S ODYSSEY

### "PILOTING ALASKA"-tm

San Francisco, Paris, New York, Southerness, Santa Fe

# ANGEL'S DIAMONDS

## Wayne Pinger

*firefall*<sup>tm</sup>

First Edition: April 2018
hardcover: 978-1-939434-739
paper-bound: 978-1-939434-746
ebook: 978-1-939434-753
audiobook: 978-1-939434-760

**Library of Congress Cataloging-in-Publication Data**

Names: Pinger, Wayne, author.
Title: Angel's diamonds : piloting Alaska / Wayne Pinger.
Description: First edition. | San Francisco : Firefall, 2018.
Identifiers: LCCN 2017046143| ISBN 9781939434739 (hardcover) | ISBN
  9781939434746 (softcover)
Subjects:  LCSH: Air pilots--Alaska--Fiction.
Classification: LCC PS3616.I568 A85 2018 | DDC 813/.6--dc23
LC record available at https://lccn.loc.gov/2017046143

*firefall originals*-tm

literary@att.net
www.firefallmedia.com

SPECIAL THANKS to my wife Jeanette for putting up with my many rereads and, alternately, my lack of response when writing overly preoccupied me; to Horace Black my Alaskan Flight Instructor; and to Jack O Brian; a very real person. Also special thanks to Carrie Ferguson, my daughter in law, for reading the first chapter and encouraging me to write thirty-two more.

# Chapter One

## — DELIVERY —

JOSH BROWNING rolled his black and gold Cessna 185 slowly left in order to view the length of the gravel bar, his landing area. With thirty degrees of flaps he was flying slow and low: barely on the front end of the power curve, just hanging on the prop but still flying. At about fifty feet over the water he planned to overfly the bar and see if one of the occasional spring time floods had deposited any new obstacles in the path of his oversize twenty inch Tundra tires where he'd be landing. The sandbar was short with a few fresh pieces of woody debris but nothing that looked dangerous to his tires.

A newly grounded willow, still green, a sweeper, lay far off to the right of the river flow. The willow was just another victim of the sporadic springtime floods that constantly eroded the banks of the Coleville River on its journey north to the Harrison Bay on the Beaufort Sea. Every year the river changed course: over the eons, slowly moving east, then slowly west, constantly changing its shape but never changing its direction or character.

If the river continued to drift east, the willow might survive. It would try to reestablish some of its old root system and new growth would emerge from the horizontal trunk and turn toward the sky. The Willow might recover and thrive: or it might become just another sweeper trying for a short time, to impede the human river traffic.

Josh dragged the gravel bar just once: he had no spare tire and a blowout on landing might be disastrous. The plane's cargo was a pallet of R&R Canadian Whiskey: 672 bottles, a little over 1,000 pounds. He was close to the 1,600 pound gross weight listed in the Cessna Specs.: 225 lbs for Josh, 300 lbs for fuel and some emergency gear: that was about all the plane could carry.

Josh had taken out the duel controls to save a few lbs. He usually left in the right hand front seat because he'd sometimes haul a passenger for one of the Master Guides in the area.

But this time it was gone because of the weight and balance specifications and the need to distribute the cargo. The rear seats were also gone as that space was for cargo only. Josh had devised a way to quickly take out the front seat by pulling two small pins from the seat tracks, so he could quickly load or unload the plane without the need to work around the right front seat. Josh wished he had a Cessna 206, maybe next year. A Cessna 206 came with a really large cargo door.

He mainly hauled to the villages and a few rural mining operations: cargo never talked back or asked stupid questions, and cargo never ever got air sick. He seldom carried passengers for hire except for the Guides, so there was no static between him and the air taxi operators. Josh had delivered many loads before, but delivering booze to river bars was pretty new, and he hoped it'd be a continuing money maker.

The trip from Fairbanks burned off about 25 gallons of fuel, 160 pounds or so. Josh was a little below gross now and with no obstacles on either end of the mid-river bar as he dragged in low and slow, just above stall, hanging on the prop. It wasn't hard to put the Cessna in smooth but he still might have trouble getting it stopped.

The R&R whiskey was not thought to be high quality, but the container made it the beverage of choice for the Pipe Line workers. The plastic rectangular one liter bottles fit easily in the pocket of most jackets and parkas: it was perfect for carrying, sharing, and sipping.

Because of a few recent brawls and one really bad one, that sent four Pipe Liners to the hospital, Alyeska had set up new security check points at Atigun Pass in an attempt to keep camps on the North Slope dry: good luck with that one. These check points were stopping a lot of the booze coming in by truck, but since the pipe line workers were very willing to pay for their enjoyment, other transportation options were utilized. That's where Josh and Goldstream Air Services came in, and that's why he was on one of his few trips north. Josh felt like he was getting away with something illegal but in fact he was breaking no law. Alyeska was probably in violation of free trade laws: but that's another story.

It's true that truckers were still bringing in a few bottles of booze and a few pounds of Happy Weed but their delivery costs were going up and the camps up north of the pass were getting pretty dry. A couple of Air Taxi operators had ferried in some booze with their charter passenger service to the Alyeska strip at Coldfoot, but rumor had it that one operator had been denied landing rights just last week, because of the booze. Josh was not an air taxi operator and had no license to lose: he was just an ordinary common Alaska Bush Pilot that endured hours of flying boredom interspaced by moments of sheer terror. Besides owning and operating the Golden Valley General Store with his wife Claire, Josh made six or eight trips to the bush each month, hauling whatever someone would pay for that fit in a Cessna 185. It had been Claire's idea to separate the store from the cargo flying venture, so one would not be libel for the other. The store was making a few bucks, but in the last three months the Goldstream Air Services was a gold mine of profit.

At first his business model had barely paid its expenses: it was touch and go for awhile. But with the first booze delivery: he could hardly believe the volume of sales. It was so simple to buy a case for $54.00 and sell it delivered on a gravel bar on the Coleville River for $175.00. He had month to month credit from P&J, the wholesaler in Fairbanks, and grossed $6,700.00 per delivery. At almost one delivery per week that exceeded the normal income of the Golden Valley Store by many times. Life was getting very good for Josh and Claire. This was the tenth whiskey delivery in a dozen weeks: they could hardly believe their good luck.

The pickup riverboat and crew were already on the sand bar and standing way off to the side. At near gross he had told them he needed all the length he could get.

Because the river was running pretty high and fast, the bar was less exposed than usual on his previous deliveries. With no wind to speak of he landed up river and with forty degrees of flaps he still had a hundred feet of bar left before he'd have been baptized. He could land but wouldn't have been able to takeoff with his plane near gross weight.

On prior deliveries two guys came with the boat: this time there were three. Josh didn't know how or who paid the boat handlers but he'd always given them a couple bottles as a thank you and figured this time he might have to give up a couple more. When they approached the plane he saw that only two were Natives, the usual ones, and the third guy, the new guy, was white.

The white guy was in charge: the Indians said very little and lugged the cases from the plane to the flat bottom river-boat. The white guy did not help with the transfer but, after checking the contents of a couple of cases, quickly paid for it: cash money in neat clean one hundred dollar bills. He almost smiled once; Josh understood that this was not the highlight of his day.

As before he was told they would contact the store soon to schedule another shipment. Josh was pleased and wondered how long this gig could possibly last. When he tried to give the Indians a couple of bottles the white guy said to not do it: not necessary or wanted. He sounded harsh, like a Marine non-com talking to new Boots. Josh didn't like being talked to that way: he was surprised at the tone but this guy was the one with the money. Josh was 6' 2" and 225, he had a good three inches on him and about fifty pounds. It'd be no problem to push back a little but it was poor form to argue with the guy that controlled the money. Josh knew that he had a quick temper, about the only person that who really control him was Claire, and boy, did she ever have him twisted around her little finger.

So Josh let it slide and was happy, he had his money and was ready and eager to fly back to Goldstream Valley. The guy had a lump under his jacket that was not a sandwich, it was probably a 9mm or so Josh guessed. Josh also was armed: he had his 44 mag. revolver. He never left on a flight without it. Anyone who spent any time in the bush except a few "Bunny Huggers" was usually so equipped. Protect yourself or stay home!

Josh was surprised when the Indians jumped back in the flat bottom river boat and pushed off without the boss. It was a bit of a push as the boat was about 1,000 pounds heavier than when it arrived. The outboard motor was a 50 hp Merc and had a jet pump conversion: it started quickly and after turning around in the current it was throwing a long rooster tail but still going down river slowly: the pilot was looking for some shallow water ground effect to get the boat on the step. He soon found the shallow bar and was up on the step and gone in just a few minutes. Finally the tranquil quiet sounds of the Coleville River returned, and in spite of a few mosquitoes, it was not a bad day.

After a call on a satellite radio the white guy introduced himself as Carter Thomas. He sounded as though Josh should know the name and be impressed. He said he hailed from Houston and contracted with the "Seven Sisters" as a security consultant, the Seven Sisters were the seven major oil companies that operated worldwide. Josh thought anyone in Alaska who didn't know that was either dead or drunk, maybe both.

As Alyeska is a consortium formed by the Seven Sisters to build and operate the Trans Alaskan Pipeline, Carter's little bit of information was strange, as it seemed he was selling booze to the folks who were trying to stop the flow of booze to the North Slope. Josh noted it was also novel that Thomas worked for the Seven Sisters and not Alyeska.

As Josh was digesting this information he heard an inboard jet boat in the distance. The sound of the jet boat was north of him, running up stream and getting closer but still a mile or so away. Carter Thomas also heard the boat and said his ride would be arriving soon. He then said Josh should leave now: it wasn't a suggestion but more a command. Again the tone kind of pissed off Josh and he was about to push back when Carter apologized and said again that he'd be in touch soon and explain the situation at the next delivery. He asked how much weight Josh could haul and would Josh want to quietly haul other cargo to the gravel bar or other places. Asked him twice to think about it.

Josh, with 315 hp and twenty degrees of flap, put the nearly empty 185 in the air after about 300 ft of sand bar. Josh retracted the flaps, brought the prop back to 2350, and reduced the manifold pressure to cruise. He slowly banked south up the Coleville and decided to follow it back for a while before turning a bit to over fly Bettles. He was pretty proud of the returns of the day because after expenses he was more than $5,000.00 in the black. His wife had been after him to set up a sinking fund to buy the much wanted Cessna 206 when the 185 got old. Josh wanted both planes: a 185 can get into places that a 206 can only fly over and wish. His wife was the heavy handed frugal business person of the family: but she did treat him better than hired help—mostly.

It was almost two hours later when Josh passed to the right of Wickersham dome on the 320 degree radial of the Fairbanks VOR. He trimmed the nose down a little and in spite of the heavy drag from the twenty inch tundra tires he was making over one sixty. Turning a little East and helped by a nice tail wind in twenty minutes or so he'd be landing on the small strip behind The Ivory Exchange Restaurant that was next to the Golden Valley Store. He flew direct, not stopping in Bettles as he sometimes did. Flying low over the Golden Valley Store he exercised the prop to announce his arrival and hoped Claire planned something for dinner besides chicken. Then after making a low 180, he landed on the short strip up-hill going to the north.

Josh always said that if he landed a little long, the store

would stop him before he crashed into the gas pumps. Claire never thought that was funny. He taxied within thirty feet of the rear loading dock before shutting down the engine. Claire and Angel welcomed his arrival and Claire was eager to hear about the trip. She was more than eager to count the money. Angel greeted Josh in the way she only did for him. She stood up and put her paws on his shoulders and gave him one, only one, lick on his nose. Welcome back Josh: got any treats?

Tomorrow would be a banking day and after the bank, Josh would have to stop by Alaska Distributers to pick up a dozen cases of Coke. They had been out of coke a week ago during the normal delivery: all of it had gone to Deadhorse in Prudhoe Bay: again. After a visit to the Northward Hub and a payment to their fuel distributer in North Pole, all he had to do was pick up fifty-five canned hams and ten cases of hot-dogs at Robert's, the wholesale food and produce distributor. Fire season was in full swing and the Golden Valley Store had again bid and won the contract to supply food to State of Alaska fire fighters. The Federal Fire Fighter food contract was won by another bidder: too bad!

## CHAPTER TWO

### — THE GOLDSTREAM VALLEY —

EARLY SUMMER in the Goldstream Valley was mild and dry. Pleasant zephyrs off the nearby hills moderated the hottest days. Cooler nights were common after the sun set below the hills in front of the White Mountains to the northwest but it never got cold in the summer. Mosquitoes, that hid from the sun during the day, came out in masses after sunset. Swallows and even a few bats scooted and swooped after the swarms of mosquitoes. It was never very  dark in the summer months, just as it never got all that bright at high noon in the winter.

The single most prominent landmark in the Valley is the Ivory Exchange Restaurant. It's one of the better eateries in the Fairbanks area and not only does it have class, it also has a pool room lounge with two tables and a satellite TV link with a rear projection big screen TV, just adjacent to the bar. The Exchange, as it's called, is nine miles north of Fairbanks, right in the middle of the Goldstream Valley.

The Ivory Exchange managed to attract many customers year round. In the summer tourist season a reservation was usually needed on Friday nights through the weekend. Ivory Skip Davis built the restaurant, but Don Peters and Tommy Wilson, the valley's first official and openly gay couple, now own and operate it.

Ivory Skip, or Skip, as he is now called, also built the Golden Valley General Store, next door to The Exchange. The General Store is a grocery and liquor store, a gas station, and a laundromat (Soapies). Originally Skip sold it to a couple of professors from the University who thought they were business men. General Store proprietors they were not. Josh and his wife Claire, had bought it from them.

In his younger days Skip flew out to the villages and purchased or traded for ivory. Skip is big, bold and has endless energy. He's a bigger than life guy even today. When he was younger he could go in several directions at once and had the vision to just plain know what a customer wanted. Actually he'd sold ice boxes to Eskimos: or rather traded iceboxes for ivory.

Skip at 6'1" is almost as large as Josh. Skip has broad shoulders and a narrow hip but is now starting to get a little gray and maybe a little belly, just a little. He has jet black hair and a full black, but now graying, beard. Skip possesses a commanding deep voice that gives him the sound and also the appearance of ageless wisdom and authority.

Josh smiled as he recalled just how the loud sometimes profane Skip Davis gets totally cowered by Claire, Josh's wife. She has him by the short and curlies and everyone knows it, even Skip. His latest business adventure is comprised of owning and operating, a high end bar, The Gold Bar and Lounge, in the now oil booming city of Fairbanks.

After a hip replacement and a divorce, he's slowed down just a little. Skip seems to know everything that's going on worth knowing. Sometimes he'll show up at the Golden Valley Store for just a cup of coffee, there is always a pot brewing, and he enjoys spreading the local gossip. He's worth listening to, or asking advice from. Skip and Josh were friends from the start: Josh learned that Skip is totally, completely loyal to his friends: Josh would trust him with most anything.

The folks at Dave's log cabin building operation across the road from the store work some twelve hours a day in the summer: most have the good sense to leave for the lower 48 in the winter when thirty below is a bit cold for outside work.

The Goldstream Valley is a sled dog paradise of kennels. It seems that the two best places to have a kennel in the Fairbanks area is either Chena Hot Springs Road or the Goldstream Valley. There's also a bunch of kennels in the North Pole area which is about fourteen miles south of Fairbanks, down the Richardson Hwy.

During the winter there is sled dog racing on most weekends. The Mushers Association on Farmers Loop Road has a nice track but the best races are the cross country contests. The most famous is the Iditarod but the toughest one is the Yukon Quest. The Quest starts in Whitehorse, Yukon Territory, and the musher's race about 1,000 miles to Fairbanks. The next year they turn it around and race back to Whitehorse. The thing that makes the Quest hard is that the mushers have to carry everything they need for the trip, including food, on their sleds. The race to Nome, the Iditarod, lets the musher's stock pile the food and supplies along the way: not that it's an easy race, it's not.

But it's a different kind of race and most mushers agree that the Yukon Quest is about the toughest organized contest now going on: anywhere. Both the Iditarod and the Quest bring in mushers from all over the world once a year to Anchorage and Fairbanks. The Quest can go as long as fourteen days and always starts on the same day regardless of the weather.

Not everyone with sled dogs races them though. A lot of the Goldstream mushers hook up their dogs on the weekends and have family outings or club picnics, or maybe a potluck after a little trail ride for the kids. The dogs seem to like the pulling, although the Golden Valley Store's guard dog Angel, would argue that she's never pulled and never will pull a sled: she might pull a sled if Claire asked her to, maybe.

The sled dogs in the neighborhood, and there are hundreds of them, mostly have the summer off. There are a few adamant, mostly newer, mushers who have their dogs pulling wheeled sleds in the summer. It might seem like a good idea for training but a good racing dog, if working hard, might overheat or pull the pads right off its feet in the summer. Some folks say the snow in winter cools the dog's feet and keep their foot pads healthy. Most folks agree however, it's just plain wrong to see sled dogs pulling wheeled carts in the summer with no snow, just plain wrong!

There are many more sled dogs in the Goldstream Valley

than people and they all have to be fed. The store does a good business selling dry dog food to the folks who have smaller kennels. The larger kennels with a hundred or so dogs usually buy dry food in bulk directly from the producers.

Sometimes it seems that almost everyone either races dogs or wants to: but not everyone. Josh and Claire own a female German Sheppard, Angel. Angel was a drug sniffing dog once, with the Seattle police department, Drug enforcement Division. She was retired at the old age of seven and is far from being "long in the tooth". She's a very smart dog: Angel is the security system for the store and knows her job well. She doesn't allow anyone on the front porch of the store until Claire or Josh open the door for business. Angel will raise her hackles, lower her head, and growl lowly at most anyone not known to her who might try to walk up the steps onto the porch before the doors open at 9:00am.

There was a time however, when Angel cowered. One of the more unique of the local Smith Road residents, Robert Foxworthy, came by the store early to buy a pack of smokes. A recent transplant from the Amazon River basin, he claimed to have been a Peace Corp worker. Almost no one believed him: most folks thought he'd never worked for the Peace Corp and maybe he had just plain never worked at all. Robert was just a big lazy guy who had a real talent for showing up at dinner time and somehow getting invited to the table. He'd usually have some gossip that folks absolutely positively needed to know and they'd have to pry it out of him with a meal.

Robert owned a pet parrot: a Hyacinth Macaw. This bird was bright almost metallic blue and nearly three feet tall. The parrot was riding on Robert's shoulder that day. He arrived a little early, before the doors were open. When Angel saw the parrot she turned tail, ran for cover, hid under the loading dock behind the store, and had to be bribed to come out with a stick of jerky. Angel does not like parrots and she won't say why: of course Angel doesn't say much about anything.

Robert was just one of many fairly strange local folks in the Goldstream Valley. A lot of folks lived off the electric grid: some because they liked the life style, some due to necessity. There were a few "End of the Roaders" and these were the guys and gals who Angel really kept an eye on: except if they had a Macaw.

The Valley was hardly the end of the road but just the same it seemed to attract some very unique people. Ivory Skip Davis guessed that fully one quarter of the Valley folks had lower 48 warrants out against them: he may've been correct. Josh and Claire were probably the most normal of all and not all that "run of the mill" themselves.

The Golden Valley Store did not accept food stamps. It was not an overwhelming moral decision: it was a paperwork thing and Josh did not like paperwork. Claire got stuck with the books and the book keeping and thought food stamps were not for the Golden Valley Store.

Yet a lot of the Valley folks who got food stamps still seemed to have money to shop at the store. It was rumored that one of the pawn shops in Fairbanks paid fifty cents on the dollar for the stamps and one of their employees would drive out to the valley early in the month for the buy.

A couple of Graduate Students at the University had a "borrowed" Xerox color copier that could make some pretty good copies of food stamps. They printed and passed a few and the proceeds of these sales pretty much paid the food and booze bills for some pretty wild Friday night parties at an "A Frame Lodge" near the Ester Dome ski area. The ski area was high up on the hill above the famous gold mining town of Ester just a little east of Fairbanks. The counterfeit stamp sales stopped dramatically quick after one of the student "stamp guys" got beat up and told to get out of the counterfeiting business. Pawn shops do not like being ripped off. After that the parties were less often and they were usually "Bring your own Bottle" affairs.

The greater Fairbanks area in the 1970s was a boom town. Pipe line money and Pipe Liners were taking a toll on the area and the culture was changing. Strangely, most of the folks, the locals, didn't seem to even notice or if they did, didn't seem to care. Life went on for the locals much as usual except prices went up on most everything and there was total employment.

The School System in Fairbanks was substandard and the Lathrop High School students were on half day sessions for several years in the early 1970s. A lot of high school students found part time employment in town when the adults left for work on the North Slope.

The Goldstream store was less affected by the oil boom than most other businesses in the greater Fairbanks area. This did not include the whiskey delivery business in which Josh was really making a buck. Claire went about improving and tweaking the business plan for the store as she learned what worked and what didn't. There were many other matters, some immediate, to tend to at the store.

The Packman video game in the laundromat was swallowing quarters again and pretending it wasn't. Josh solved that one by pulling the plug and putting an "out of order" sign on it. Another nasty call to the Video game supplier pleading for a better machine went unanswered: again. The water softener in "Soapies", the store's laundromat, worked most of the time, but not all of the time. Josh would sometimes question if owning the store was really worth the agony. He wondered today why he came back to the valley as quickly as he did. Josh thought of himself as a pilot, not a store keeper: he was yearning for the wild blue more and more.

The Wednesday night poker game would be starting at 7:00 pm down the road at Ralph Sims' house. Ralph never won much but God knows he tried. The players all thought he just wanted the visitors: and the visitors thought he needed to shower a little more often. Ralph mined gold north of Fairbanks in the Livengood Mining District. During the summer he made a decent living on his one-man operation and it was suspected maybe he salted away a few hundred extra ounces for his old age. When the mining operation was working in the summer, Ralph drove the sixty miles back to the Valley every Wednesday just for the poker game, did his weekly shopping on Thursday and after dinner and a quickie with his girlfriend, drove back to Livengood. Ralph was older than most, maybe around sixty. Ralph had some interesting stories to tell: some were even true.

He'd started mining antimony with Earl Pilgrim at the Stampede Mine near the back end of Denali Park in the 1940s. The mine was now dormant: Earl said he was waiting for commodity prices to go up before reopening it. Not very likely, since Earl was now in his 80s and the surrounding areas were being scooped up to increase the size of Denali Park: like it really needs to be bigger.

Pretty soon the mine will be an in-holding in the park and getting permits to reopen the mining operation will be next to impossible. Earl Pilgrim once sat in on one of the weekly poker games and bought chips with Silver Certificate Dollar bills. Earl was a bad poker player as anyone at that game might tell you but somehow he won a lot of money with bad play and a few lucky hands.

A few of the folks who lived up on Smith Road cultivated and utilized "Happy Weed". A few of the folks were almost perpetually stoned. Claire thought it permanently affected at least some of them: or all of them. There was of course no smoking in the store and Clair asked if maybe there could be no smoking of Pot up wind of the store: fat chance.

Of the thirty or forty families that lived up Smith Road maybe half were patrons of the store. Like most Alaskans they just wanted to live and let live: pretty good folks.

# CHAPTER THREE

*— ANOTHER DELIVERY, A LITTLE MYSTERY —*

THE NEXT TUESDAY a call came for another delivery of R&R. The caller again wanted a full pallet, to be paid for on delivery. Claire found that this was a little illegal, because according to Alaska liquor laws: other than wholesale any delivered liquor must be paid for at the point of sale, which had to be at the address on the "off sale" license. Surprisingly, the caller had no objection to this and said the money would be delivered to the store the next day. Claire would be happy with that one and Josh would be less worried about being robbed or carrying so money around after the delivery on the sand bar. It had happened to other folks before, but not yet to Josh.

Early morning the next day a semi-bald-headed mousy looking guy arrived by the name of Pete, just Pete, with no last name that he would admit to. Josh had seen him before somewhere around town but could not remember where. He arrived with $6,700.00 cash: the crisp new hundred dollar bills were in, believe it or not, a plain brown envelope. He also gave Josh a larger package to deliver. It was about the size of a loaf of bread and well taped up: Pete said it was very important that it be delivered to the same gravel bar as the last delivery. Josh wondered: where the hell else would he deliver it? As before Pete asked Josh to call and say when the delivery could be made so they could schedule the pickup boat. Josh said he was pretty sure that the delivery would be sometime early on Friday or Saturday. That was fine and dandy with Pete.

Josh needed to pick up some needed produce at Robert's and decided to drive over and see the manager at P&J distributors in person to order another pallet of R&R whiskey. Dick the manager, was happy to see the order and asked Josh where the market for this liquor was. Usually if one retailer orders more, another retailer will order less. Dick said that the market had been growing rather steadily, but the amount that the Golden Valley Store was ordering was still unusual. The market that Josh seemed to be supplying, whatever it was, must have previously been wholesaled from another market: maybe Anchorage.

Dick: "I know this is none of my business but I think you should be aware that two FBI special Agents were here a couple of weeks ago: they asked about these added whiskey sales. It's strange because ATF should be asking if anything is going on with liquor sales. They asked that I not mention this to anyone but the more I think about it the more I wonder if they were really who they said they were."

Josh: "Who do you think they might be?"

Dick: "Not a clue"

Josh: "Who'd even know how much you were supplying, how much you were selling to who?"

Dick: "Maybe the shippers or the transfer agents: that's all I can think of. I will let you know if I find out anything more but it's strange and thought you might like to know"

Josh: "Thanks, when do you think the product can be delivered?"

Dick said the whiskey, the R&R, would arrive at the store directly from the North Star Terminal on Thursday or Friday and this really pleased him because he got his markup and never had to handle the merchandise. Business folks might not have liked the wages demanded by the Teamsters but they did like the way that the Teamsters operated. If the merchandise was to be delivered it'd be delivered: on time, secure, with only a small percent missing (shrinkage, it's called).

The Pipeline Construction had changed the casual Alaska business culture. The term "Typical Alaska Operation" now no longer described the way business was run in or near Fairbanks. Before the pipeline you promised what you hoped would happen. Now, if you wanted to stay in business, you said what you would do, and then did what you said.

One good thing the pipeline did was to bring business

practices in urban Alaska into the Twenty First Century. And one of the worst things the construction did was to bring urban Alaska into the Twenty First Century.

Since construction started folks found it necessary to lock their houses when leaving, take care to remove their car keys when parking, and maybe not to pick up hitch hikers. Alaska culture had changed, and most folks admitted it was probably forever.

After the money arrived, Josh flew over to Northwinds Aviation at Fairbanks International (FIA) to gas up the plane. Aviation gas, 100 octane low lead, was up to over a buck a gallon and nobody was happy about the rip-off. Later that day Josh noticed one tire on the 185 needed air so, he filled it. The engine didn't require extra oil which was a pleasant surprise, but Josh noticed one of the two landing lights wasn't working. They were expensive to replace: he planned to schedule the work at Northwinds Aviation later next week.

Josh made a call to the FAA Flight Service Station and inquired about the forecast at Bettles. The weather report was maybe OK on Saturday and maybe marginal on Friday; Josh decided he'd try to make the delivery Saturday morning. He called the number of his now favorite customer to schedule the whiskey drop-off on the gravel bar on the Colville River for Saturday, late morning.

The day was ending: Claire decided to close a little early and gave her head clerk Jean, the rest of the day off. It was only about 1:45 minutes early but still a nice gesture that Jean appreciated. Josh called Angel inside and, after locking the front door, walked into the liquor section of the store and picked out a bottle of wine to have with dinner. When he was readying to lock up the back door by the loading dock, Angel growled. Josh looked out and saw a well-dressed fellow walking around his 185, looking at it. Josh thought maybe the guy was an early customer for The Ivory Exchange Restaurant next door. Sometimes folks from the Exchange wandered through the Goldstream Store to shop for the more unique Native Crafts that the store retailed.

The markup on quality Native Crafts was huge, around 300%, and shelf space requirement was minimal. Claire didn't sell the "Crap" from Korea, China, or places like that. She didn't even like to retail the ivory that came out of Nome because most of it was "Assembly line" stuff from a semi-famous bar where local artists would trade their talent for carving ivory to satisfy their booze addiction. So it wasn't strange to see tourists walking around the area and Josh said, Hi. The guy asked if Josh was a Bush Pilot and lots of questions about his delivery services. He sounded like a typical tourist except he seemed to know a little something about flying. Did he supply Gold Camps? Did he fly fisherman into great fishing areas? Would he fly tourists around the Fairbanks area for photographs? Yes, no and, no. Josh just hated flying live cargo and the local Air Taxi Operators were really hostile to cargo pilots who did. They thought it was their part of the aviation business and folks like Josh should not interfere or otherwise enter their domain. Josh had always maintained a good business relationship with the Air Taxis, and some of the operators would on occasion send him some business. Angel was not as convinced as Josh that everything was fine, and really gave the guy a good sniffing. She tried to stay between Josh and the curious tourist and only calmed down after the guy departed. Josh locked the 185, something he seldom did and walked up the stairs for dinner.

Dinner was classical Claire cuisine: roast chicken, rice, and white wine. Dessert was apple pie, also out of one of the freezers in the store. Claire had said, when they considered whether or not to buy the store, that win or lose, they could always get a decent meal out of the freezers. Josh wondered what the exact definition of a decent meal was, though he kept his question to himself.

While Claire cleaned the table and stuffed the garbage can with the paper plates from dinner Josh turned on the

TV to get the news of the day. It was announced, on the best of the three channels available, that the daily news tapes from Seattle didn't arrive on time so yesterday's news would be rebroadcast. That was a "Typical Alaska Operation" thing that did not seem to change during "operation pipeline".

Later while looking through the business books, Claire asked Josh if he was leaning the mixture enough on his recent flights. She said fuel costs were higher than usual. Josh wondered but didn't ask, if she was going to back-seat fly just like she always back-seat drove in their van.

When driving Josh was never without the knowledge of the speed limit, whether he was driving too close to the center line, where he should park, and exactly how long it should take to go from here to there. When he said he hated to haul passengers, he sometimes included his life partner as a passenger: both in a car and in a plane. But flying, Claire was a very good navigator, and Josh appreciated that.

Josh sat in his old but sturdy recliner sipping the last of the wine and feeling quite proud of himself in regards to his flying. Saturday he'd put another $6,000.00 of profit on the books and might even take a day off to fish grayling on the Chatanika. A fishing day was unpaid leave for the self-employed and Josh already felt guilty just thinking about fishing. But then he thought he might find some fish on the Coleville during his booze delivery on Saturday. He'd have to remember to put his fly rod in the plane and forget to mention fishing to Claire.

# CHAPTER FOUR

## — SATURDAY DELIVERY —

SATURDAY MORNING SAW Josh loading the 185. The pallet of booze, being fifty-six cases, took up a bunch of space, but the right seat was out because, although the Cessna can haul the weight, there's also a weight distribution problem. The balance and weight chart for the plane indicated that eighteen cases had to be placed forward of the back seats. Also the cargo had to be secured so it doesn't move around if turbulence is encountered during the flight. Josh is fairly cautious compared to many of the Bush Pilots now flying, as he fully intends to have a long and happy life. He is happy to do things right, or nearly so, most of the time.

At thirty-six, he's almost "old age" among his peers: some refer to him as "The Old Man". Josh says he's a damn young, old man, and if you question him he might challenge you to a little Arm Wrestling match: for maybe $100.00. No one has stepped up yet and probably no one will.

Josh is not well known outside of Fairbanks. After Military training he flew out of Nome and Bristol Bay, and put a bunch of hours in his log book in South Eastern flying many different aircraft. One of his favorite gigs was flying supplies into and fish out of some of the best fishing resorts in the world in a Dehavilland Beaver, out of the Juneau Douglass area.

He had also flown a French Alouette helicopter out of Yakutat for one season, where he met Claire who taught math temporarily at the high school there. Claire was an out of work Geologist turned school teacher: at least until she could find a better job.

The Hubbard Glacier, up Yakutat bay, was one of the Seven Wonders, according to Josh: he loved to fly over it and the Variegated Glacier also, across the bay from the Hubbard. Once he'd flown Claire, out to Variegated Glacier for a picnic. They picnicked on the lower moraine, to watch the Hubbard

Glacier calving icebergs as large as small skyscrapers into the bay. The bergs caused huge waves to break across Osier Island. They occasionally swamped a grounded fishing trawler that had been left high and dry, destroyed, by the tidal wave from the 1964 Anchorage Earthquake. Flying a Helicopter was a decent job but after his marriage to Claire, who thought Southeast was too wet and foggy, he looked for employment flying in a more normal environment. He tried Interior Alaska: hardly normal temperatures but at least dry and clear usually. Not able to find Aviation work in Fairbanks he took a year off from flying and taught math at Lathrop High in Fairbanks. His BS in General Science let him qualify for the position.

Teaching paid OK but he missed flying. With the pipeline construction starting, through a friend Josh was offered a job with AIA, Alaska International Air, as a copilot on a C130 Hercules (A Herkeybird). Claire said to "go for it" but Josh didn't like the schedule, or the duty, nor was there much adventure flying a 4 engine turboprop. He and Claire, who was substitute teaching PE at Lathrop High now, considered a job with Era Aviation in Nome, Charter Flying a Twin Turboprop Otter. If Era Aviation had employed Claire in their office he might've accepted the job, but instead, and almost on a whim, Josh and Claire put a down payment on the Golden Valley General Store: and also a used, but pretty sturdy, Cessna 185 Skywagon.

They had no business plan, just lots of energy, and Claire had a good amount of business sense. At first there was a god awful large monthly payment, including a second mortgage, but the second is finally paid off and it's not as tight as it was for a while. Also, with a mysterious new whiskey customer they now pull off what most of their friends said would be next to impossible to do.

After the preflight and saying his "So Longs" to Claire and Angel, Josh pushed the tail around, got in, buckled up, and fired the engine. The morning was cool and crisp and visibility seemed to be CAVU: "Ceiling and Visibility Unlimited". Josh could see the Alaska Range to the south as though it were a mile away instead of ninety miles in reality. Mt McKinley was not up as far as usual, when it had atmospheric inversion: just the same it looked magnificent and took up a large part of the south western sky. Josh dialed in takeoff trim and hardly touched the yoke as the 185 left the ground. Right rudder trim was already adjusted in and he left it there as he pulled back the prop to 2350 RPM: his cruise pitch. Bringing back the manifold pressure to 23" of HG at 500 ft AGL "Altitude above the Ground", he checked the amp meter and oil temp and pressure, and the vacuum pump. Josh banked slightly left and continued a lazy gain of altitude as he crossed over the intersection of Balliane Rd. and Goldstream Valley Rd. He needed just a little more altitude to over-fly Clary Summit on the Steese, and from there it was a heading of 314 magnetic and about 160 nautical miles to Wiseman: from there another 128 miles on the same heading to the sand bar on the Colville. Having flown the route before, he knew the numbers. After crossing Clary Summit, Josh climbed to 7,000 ft and enjoyed a little tail wind. At his slow cruise he'd still be an hour early and might have time to wet his fly line. He leaned out the engine a little, just a little rich of peak and reset the gyro compass with the magnetic one. The plane felt heavy on take-off but was making knots now. The air was very smooth and he fiddled with the trim till it was perfect. Life was great!

About sixty miles past Wiseman Josh dropped the nose of the 185 a little and the speed went almost to the Red line: 180 knots. The air was smooth and even at 4,000 ft and shirt sleeve temperature. Josh was already thinking about the bug repellent and what fly pattern he would cast for the grayling he hoped to catch. When he spotted the familiar bend in the Coleville from 10 miles away, he slowed the Cessna down. Ten minutes later with the prop in takeoff pitch he was 100 feet above the river and had the plane slowed to eighty knots as he passed over the bar for the first time. Josh overflew the bar once to see if anything new was there to ruin a tire.

As he flew by low, he noticed the pickup boat already on the beach. The crew seemed to be missing but the boat was there on the bar: no one at all was on the river bar. He turned 180 finally from about half a mile down river and slowed to just above stall with 40 degrees of flaps. Still, Josh landed a little long: he was distracted by the boat, and the warmer day let his 185 float too much in ground effect. When he finally got the plane stopped, the main gear was within 25 feet of the water's edge.

He got out of the plane. Walking back up the bar he was surprised to notice that the flat bottom riverboat had a few well placed bullet holes in its bottom and two in the power-head of the Merc 500 outboard motor. The crew was nowhere to be found, and he wondered if he was into a new adventure. Then he spotted what looked like wet blood on the gunnels of the boat, and a little more blood near the water's edge.

# CHAPTER FIVE

## — BULLET HOLES AND BAD GUYS —

The bullet holes, and especially the blood, reminded Josh of his two years in Nam: the memories weren't pleasant.

Investigating he looked and found no shell casings, but did find two, or maybe three, new sets of foot prints on the sand bar. Josh thought that it was, well, he didn't know what to think, but wondered if whoever shot up the boat, and maybe its passengers, was still in the area: what the hell had gone on here?

Then Josh noticed small tire tracks with a tread pattern on the bar. His tundra tires had no pattern: they were high floatation and bald and larger. These were not his tracks. Flying in, he hadn't noticed any traffic on the river but wasn't really looking for any either, as he was almost an hour early for the transfer. After he'd spotted the bar, the landing was all he'd worried about: the bar was getting pretty short and he was really loaded.

He'd planned to fish a little, but fishing was far from his mind now. Josh decided to wait till the appointed time before worrying more. He walked back to the plane and unloaded some of the booze. Josh had a big problem, he could not take off fully loaded. He'd have to leave at least half the whiskey if no one showed up. The chances of getting the plane off the bar fully loaded were slim to none, but he felt a real desire to exit the area: it was a flash back to his days in Nam and he did not like the feeling.

Josh waited two hours beyond the appointed time for the pickup before he heard the sound of a jet boat in the distance: he instinctively felt for his side arm. Josh had checked and rechecked it several times in the last hour. He pulled it to a-gain check the cylinder of his S&W 629 for rounds. It was full of course, six rounds. He had a dozen extra 44 Magnums and a few 44 Specials in a Crown Royal pouch stored behind the front seat of the 185. He shoved the pouch in his back pocket.

He'd no idea who was in the jet boat, he guessed it had to be Carter but, since discovering the shot up flat bottom, Josh was less sure of anything. He wondered if there'd be a pick-up at all and decided to find a little cover and pretend to fish when the jet boat got close, and if it passed by he'd just wave: if it stopped he'd figure out what was going on, one way or another. He quickly put the fly rod together and waited by the Willow snag next to the river bank.

As he stooped down behind the grounded Willow, the only limited cover, he questioned the wisdom of delivering booze to a gravel bar on the Colville River but decided to have that conversation with himself on a later date. The willow was thick enough to breakup his outline. He thought he'd have the advantage of surprise for at least a minute. Josh was Sharp Shooter qualified with a rifle but wasn't all that good with a revolver. An eight inch barreled S&W 44 wasn't the best long range defense weapon anyway, but it'd have to do.

The 44 magnum was the handgun of choice for most of the folks traveling the bush, a good short range bear gun, but its eight inch barrel seemed too big most of the time. Right then and there Josh decided that on any other trips he'd also bring his 270 Winchester rifle. The 44 was fine for Dirty Harry in the back streets of San Francisco, but without a director to say "cut", Josh wasn't feeling all that secure. Squatting behind the downed willow he wondered how Claire and Angel were doing, what she'd do when he was late, how long she'd wait until the call to Flight Services. He always completed paperwork for a flight plan, but almost never filed it. He just left it, as usual, with Claire so if he didn't return when planned he'd at least have supplied a map of his probable route and the site of his wreckage.

Claire did what store keepers generally do. Stock shelves, reorder supplies, and make customers happy. Angel was busy sleeping on the front porch behind the rocker in her typical guard dog stance. That sneaky little Pete guy, who looked so much like a rat, had just pulled into the parking lot. He'd a scent of drugs all over him: the same drugs Angel had been trained to sniff out in Seattle. She found out after months at the store that bunches of the Goldstream Valley locals smoked a lot of pot. They were nice to her, but because of her police training she rejected the friendship of the "druggies". She'd try to point out the druggies to Claire and Josh, but they wouldn't notice or worse, ignored her. Her diligence went unrewarded, no one appreciated her scrutiny, and there were no treats for a job well done. There was no reason to wake up for Pete. What a tough world it had become: sometimes she missed the Seattle rain.

The jet boat slowed down as it approached the bar. Josh saw two people in it. He kept low, wanting to see and hear these folks before they saw him. The jet boat might have no connection with the shot up riverboat, but he was pretty sure it did. The jet boat was a 21 ft. Hewes Craft Bow Rider. The open bow area was for folks to step off the front of it on to a beach and not get their feet wet.

Just at the time they grounded the boat and stepped out on the bar, Josh was attacked by the biggest swarm of Yellow Jackets he'd ever encountered. The hornets had their hive in the willow and Josh was too close: they were totally pissed off, to say the least.

Though intellectually not the right thing to do, human beings tend to react to the closer threats first: and a swarm of buzzing stinging insects is a very close and primordial threat. Somewhere, way back in the human brain is an unrelenting fear of snakes, fire, angry husbands, and bee stings. Maybe not in that order, but it's there, uncompromising.

Josh stood up, bolted toward, and then dove into the Coleville River. The new arrivals, Carter and one of the Indians, had seen the plane but were totally surprised by the Bush Pilot's rapid and nonprofessional swan dive into the Coleville.

34

After figuring out what was happening, they laughed, took the commotion in stride, and didn't get close to the hornet's nest. The laughing was loudest when they helped Josh out of the river. Josh said he was getting ready to catch a record Grayling when the hornets swarmed after him.

Carter said, "Do you have the package? How many cases of whiskey did you transport?"

Josh said "Yes, here's the package: I brought a full pallet again. The folks at P&J think I'm their best retailer."

Carter concerned himself with the shot up damaged flat bottom but didn't want to discuss it. Josh had no understanding of what the hell happened. To him it seemed very expensive vandalism. He said the Troopers should be called in and a report filed.

Carter said, Bunny Huggers had been bothering him and his crew: they probably chased his crew off and destroyed the boat. They were the Anti-Pipe Line folks who'd harassed the pipe line project since it started years ago.

Carter said, They're a pain in the butt but bringing in the law would be more work and he did not need that now: he said to let it slide.

Josh didn't buy that explanation, not for a minute, but was less worried now about his personal safety. He still had his 44 strapped on and Josh noticed that Carter and his one man crew were unarmed except for a pump shotgun in the boat. The pilot of the jet boat was the bigger of the two Indians Josh had seen before, a big man, a little younger than Josh. The Indian suggested that they push the flat bottom out onto the Coleville and let it sink. Josh said that made no sense and again that they should report the incident to the Troopers. Carter might've known what had happened on the river bar a few hours earlier, or not. But it was obvious he didn't want the law involved, now or ever. Whatever was happening was at least profitable for the Golden Valley General Store, and Josh decided that's mostly what mattered anyway.

Before leaving Carter asked, "Can you take this lock box back with you? An associate will pick it up later today, or tomorrow at your store. Please take care of it, don't misplace it, there are fairly important papers in it."

Hearing the associate's description, Josh remembered Pete, the mousey looking guy who had brought him the payment for the whiskey and the other package.

Josh said, "Sure I'll be happy to. It'll be at the store late this afternoon or amongst the scattered wreckage somewhere along the way between here and there."

The boat driver unloaded the rest of the booze from the plane and then helped Josh push the tail of the 185 around to ready his takeoff. Carter said he might need more whiskey but not a full pallet, and, if it was delivered as requested, he'd pre-pay for the booze and an extra $700.00 as a delivery fee for an extra small package, or maybe two.

Josh said, "Ok, fine, whatever.

He knew what he'd heard wasn't the full truth and decided he needed an hour of "fly rod time" to work it out.

After the jet boat left the bar going north, in the direction it came from, Josh relieved himself on the far side of the river bar. He drained a pint of gas from one of the wing tanks, threw the gas on the hornet's nest and, from a good distance, struck a match. He wanted no more bees on later trips. Then he found his fly rod and got serious about a few Grayling for the folks back home. Both Tommy and Don really liked fresh Grayling and Josh decided to bring them a few. After catching six fish and losing a couple of flies to snags, he cleaned the fish and packed them in his cool chest. He ate some jerky, drained a Pepsi, fired up the 185, and was in the air within 300 ft, into a nice breeze.

He took off south. Instead of heading directly for Bettles and home, he turned north and flew down the river for twenty miles. He'd been there before and expected to see a rundown trapper's cabin, an outhouse, a high cache, and not much else, except a very short airstrip on a nearby mud bar that only a skilled bush pilot could get into with a Super Cub or similar plane. The last time he saw the strip, a few small willows were sprouting on the mud bar/air strip and the cabin was in need of a door, a roof, and windows. What he saw now was a real surprise, and the mystery grew in his mind.

Meanwhile, Claire came out of the store onto the front porch to water the flowers in the planters, to see Pete. Claire heard Angel growl quietly and wondered why the dog was so concerned about this little guy. He was pleasant enough and, maybe because of his size, seemed no threat. Besides that, he had brought them a bunch of business, hence a bunch of money, and usually seemed friendly enough.

Claire said Hi and exchanged pleasantries. Pete asked if Josh was back yet and, if not, when was he planning to arrive. Claire said in the early afternoon she thought. She invited Pete to sit inside for coffee but he declined the offer and instead said he'd catch a sandwich and beer at the Ivory Exchange next door. Claire warned him about Tommy's pool skills and suggested he not play pool with him for money. Claire said that she'd send Angel to let him know when Josh got back. Pete hurried to the Exchange, and Claire seemed to sense he wanted to play pool with Tommy really badly. Poor Pete!

Josh saw, where the old cabin should've been on the west side of the Coleville, an 1800 foot landing strip and several new building plus a dock in a recently dugout lagoon off the side of the river. A real dock with two jet boats tied up: was he dreaming? Also, a few quads (4 wheelers) and small trailers parked near some fuel storage tanks. The dock had to be new because the winter ice would've taken out a permanent dock in the winter. The jet boats looked the same kind Carter had used. Josh wondered why he'd been asked to deliver the booze to a sand bar instead of this longer new strip. He flew fairly low, knowing he'd be seen and heard from the new air strip. He made no effort to hide.

There was a fairly wide trail away from the airstrip, going a half mile to an area that looked like a mining operation, maybe a strip mine. One small front end loader was feeding a fairly large sluice box and a D-4 Cat was pushing around and piling up over-burden. Two diesels driving pumps for the sluice water supply were running so hard that Josh could hear them from the plane. Then Josh recognized a pretty large settling pond as a closed circuit placer mining operation and was sure it was running on the "down low", but, if discovered, it didn't need EPA monitoring because none of the waste water from the sluice seemed to be returning to the Coleville. It sure looked like a gold mining operation, but there had never been gold production in the area. As Claire was a Geologist with a Master's degree in Mineral Exploration, he'd ask her about gold on the Coleville. She'd know for sure.

As he tried to digest the mystery mine he turned the 185 back toward Bettles, for a burger, and from there, on to Fairbanks. He wondered if the Lodge in Bettles would be open. He wanted to see a friend there too for any information about what was happening. Josh's belly was expanding a little as of late and maybe, just maybe, he should take in a little less food on his Bettles stop. Maybe a Bacon Cheeseburger should be a Regular Hamburger and Soggy Fries should be a small salad on the side, maybe.

## CHAPTER SIX

### — *THE MYSTERY SLOWLY REVEALED* —

CLAIRE TOLD him once that he'd always be slow to pick up on shady deals because he was basically a good guy who had trouble thinking like a bad guy. She said, "Please excuse the Good-guy Bad-guy comparison but that is just the way it is: live with it, Superman!"

Josh didn't find his friend in Bettles. Kevin was off to a small bush village repairing a float plane wing that stubbed a float while landing, by dipping a wing tip, and almost turning turtle. Kevin's wife, Molly, said the aileron needed a hinge repaired and Kevin was seeing to that.

Josh said, "Sorry I missed Kevin but I'll see him on my next trip in a week or so. Claire says Hi, and we hope to see you guys when you visit Fairbanks next. You've a standing invitation to overnight at the store."

Josh felt better talking to Molly but the rest of the day still really bugged him. He seemed equally puzzled by both the shot up riverboat and the mining operation just north of his whiskey drop. Josh was sure that there was nothing worth finding with a sluice on the Coleville.

The flight back to the Valley was uneventful but so smooth that Josh practiced, using only tail trim, aileron, and throttle to control the altitude and direction. Without elevator or rudder input, the 185 managed to fly just fine unless it flew through moderately turbulent air. Then it became necessary to use rudder and elevator inputs to fly properly and hold a good course. Horace Black, a friend and flight instructor, always said "Well designed aircraft fly well on their own until the pilot screws up and misdirects the adventure", or something similar. Josh couldn't remember the exact wording. Horace sometimes tried to be profound: Josh thought maybe too much so.

Now Josh overflew the store and again exercised the prop to let the unfortunate earth bound folks know of his eminent arrival: he never expected a red carpet but then again, he'd survived yet another harrowing experience in his continuing adventure. The shot up riverboat and hornet swarm occupied him. One was curious and scary and the other just scary.

When Josh taxied his 185 up near the back porch of the store, he was still just as puzzled as when he left the river bar. It had been a few hours but he was still a bit damp from his less than award winning Olympic Style dive into the river. The river sand in his shorts irritated his "manly" parts, but the Bettles Lodge Hamburger, side salad, and a Coke, had satisfied his hunger.

Angel greeted him with a nose licking but, as soon as she said her how-dos, Claire sent her to fetch Pete from the Ivory Exchange. Pete had been there all afternoon: Josh was 4 hours past due, go fetch! Tough life for a smart dog: she knew she couldn't play dumb, she'd tried it before but it got her only harsh words.

Pete came into the store and asked about the flight. They did a little small talk, but when Josh gave Pete the package he tried to pretend surprise and made a fairly big deal about looking around like someone might be watching. Josh had enough mystery for the day and was  unimpressed, like totally.

 About that time, in walked Skip Davis: Josh hadn't seen him in a while and asked if he wanted to sit and yak a bit. Skip seemed to know Pete, said Hey, and sat down next to the old wood burning stove that kept the store warm in the winter. A really big 500,000 BTU forced air oil fired furnace helped out a little then too. It might also melt a runaway glacier if one were found.

Skip patiently waited for Josh to break out the whiskey. The ritual was to get a couple of 16 oz plastic bottles of Pepsi from the cooler, then pour off a third of the soda pop and refill the bottles with Maker's Mark bourbon whiskey. This usually made for a happy thoughtful conversation period that ended up at the Ivory Exchange next door, with a game of pool. Pete begged off the booze and left with his package held tightly under his arm, his beady eyes searching for god knows what. He was no longer at ease with the situation: at least that's what he seemed to be projecting.

Skip asked Josh if he remembered Pete's trial: he'd been tried for killing his wife just three years ago. The story is that one Friday night Pete called the Paramedics at the Fire House on South Cushman and said his wife was having a bad reaction to a prescription medication. Turned out it was cocaine and not a legal drug at all. Anyway, the dosage proved to be pretty strong. She was blue, in Cardiac Arrest. Pete was giving his wife mouth to mouth resuscitation, when the Paramedics arrived, except one of the Paramedics thought Pete was holding his wife's nose closed and stopping her breathing with his mouth over hers. It'd taken the medics twenty minutes to find the house because Pete gave them the wrong address. Claimed it was a mistake caused by his panic because of his wife being in mortal distress. After a few hours in the hospital his wife did die. A week later, after an autopsy and investigation, Pete was charged with Murder. But there'd been no history of abuse, and the Paramedic admitted on the witness stand that he wasn't 100% sure of what he saw, or thought he saw, so the case fell apart. Also, Pete's wife was one of a half dozen hookers working the Pipe-liners down by the bars on Two Street. She was also a known cocaine seller and user. Neither of these facts should have mitigated the crime, but the jury heard them and let Pete go, finding him not guilty after deliberating for less than one hour. The jury must've felt sorry for him: they probably didn't know he was not only her drug supplier but also her pimp.

Josh hadn't heard the story before., but Skip seemed to know more about the inner workings of Fairbanks than most anyone and since Josh had fact checked a few of Skip's stories, and found them true, he believed this one.

With that little bit of gossip digested, the conversation drifted back to present day.

Skip asked, "How did the trip go?"

They jawed about the trip north and Josh filled him in on the events of the day including the dive into the Coleville, but, for some reason, didn't tell Skip about the mining operation twenty miles downriver from the booze delivery. Skip thought the "dash from the hornets" hilarious. There was no empathy in his laughter: only an empty "too bad" and fatherly snickers. Josh didn't like being made fun of, and he schemed to get Skip into a pool game a little later and hit him where it counted: in his money clip.

Skip had other news about two wise guys that hit town from Fargo, North Dakota. No one seemed to know them but they were loaded with cash and spending it like water running down the Chena River. Skip claimed, they dropped $3,000 in one night at Ruthie's House of Passion, down on 23rd. He said they lost another $5,000 in a card game at Jimmy's Elbow Room on Two Street. Skip assumed they were involved in a new drug distribution network and were partially responsible for the city's growing drug problems.

A lot of drugs were sold to the North Slope workers who had few or no places to spend their earnings. A lot of Operating Engineers, Welders, Laborers, and others, end up with seventy hours of pay, nearly thirty of it at time and a half, every working week. And then they have a week off with nothing to do.

The Slope was where a lot of money was paid to folks who spend it on the three traveling sins. Gambling, drugs, and prostitution were available widely across Fairbanks in the best and the poorest places. Like in any Boom Town the three sins take their toll on the workers and other folks left behind when the Boom travels to yet another innocent place.

Skip claimed he had many opportunities to get involved with both Gambling and Drug Selling, but turned down all offers. He's kept his newest venture, The Gold Bar and Lounge, free of vice and will until the day he's in the ground. How's that for drama?

Josh wondered if his whiskey deliveries added to the problems. Both Skip and Tommy had thoughts about it and said, "As long as the booze deliveries are legal it competes with the drug market and might, just might, even reduce the overall problem, maybe just a little."

Josh: "Well now that it's settled that I am in fact a good guy, let's play pool: who has a quarter for the table?"

They turned to the pool table and the tall stories started. Tommy believed just about anything Skip said. After all, Skip built the Ivory Exchange: what better proof of candor could there be?

At that very time, a couple of Gold Miners, with a small operation up near Circle Hot Springs, told stories about finding two diamonds in their sluice box at cleanup. As the story steeped, like a pot of tea, the number of stones grew, to over a dozen raw diamonds. Skip knew for sure that the men had been to Arkansas last year to visit relatives, because he bought the duos biggest Jewelry Grade nuggets to help finance their trip. He figured that they probably got a few commercial grade raw diamonds in Little Rock and were milking their own story big for all it was worth. The old farts still spread the news now about the diamonds, just like they'd spread unreal stories in years past.

The duo developed into first class local celebrities. The Summer Tourists believe just about anything, if told properly. The right story can get a person a bunch of free drinks, if the story is told quietly and slowly at the bar at the Circle Hot Springs Resort. Tourists like to seek out the "Real Sourdoughs" and love to listen to olden times. The tales are mostly harmless and some, if not all, of them have at least a  bit of reality at their core.

The story about Sun Flowers twisting their flower heads off was also a good one. The story goes, that the face of the Sun Flowers tries to follow the sun as it goes round and round. Since the Sun never sets in Circle City in the summer, the flowers eventually twist their heads off. It's one of the best stories told. The duo were always trying to better each other with taller and stranger tales. The thing about the diamonds was that the miners actually did have couple of raw diamonds: or maybe what they had was just quartz: maybe.

The story about Bigfoot had been around for a while too. A few years ago some men put a stuffed bear skin up in a tree with a painted plastic Halloween gorilla head: and then took some very blurry photos. The photos found their way to an editor of True or some other "reality" magazine. This got a more creative and hungry staff writer scripting away about tracking Bigfoot near the Circle Hot Springs, east of Circle City on the Yukon River. The reasoning went: with so few folks so far north it's not surprising that Bigfoot had lived in autonomy for so long.

Skip himself thought that he'd once seen Bigfoot taking a dump down near the turn off to Murphy Dome on the west end of the Goldstream Valley, but it turned out to be Skip's second wife: she'd been out picking Blue Berries at the time and felt the urge. Shortly after, they divorced: she never knew just why really, but the rumor was she made a bundle of bucks in the settlement.

The best story Skip ever told was about stealthy Polar Bears sneaking up on seals in a snow storm. The bears put one paw up in front of their black nose, and in the falling snow the seals couldn't see the snow white bears coming. The bears hopped along on three feet and caught all the seals they could eat. That's why they're thought to be such great hunters.

Tommy hadn't heard that one and laughed hard enough to miss an easy shot for the 15 ball in the side pocket, and also scratch. Skip was thrilled and got to enjoy one of very few free drinks from the bar: Other then with Skip, Tommy rarely if ever lost a pool game. He's a bit of a paradox. Most of his pool room opponents can't believe someone as kind and gentle as Tommy can have the pool skills of Minnesota Fats. He's so quiet and thoughtful when playing. His skill is unique: as is Tommy himself. He claims to be a very lucky player but admits that the more he practices the luckier he gets.

And so the conversation continued far into the night. At about 11:00 Angel pushed thru the door and pulled on Josh's sleeve: "time to come home and eat." Josh had forgotten dinner: he really liked visiting with Skip and Tommy. It'd been a long day and the pool game and stories made Josh almost forget about the shot up river boat and the mystery of the mine on the Coleville River.

## Chapter Seven

### — A Down Day —

SUNDAY STARTED SLOW, then got back to normal. The ice maker was putting out slush again, and something was wrong with the pilot light in the #2 dryer at Soapies, the laundromat. Josh fixed the pilot light failure with a very, very small drill and a delicate hand. Then a Maytag washer wouldn't pump the rinse water out. That made for yet another happy customer: NOT! "Look lady, just take your clothes out of number 4 and put them in number 5. Here's a token for number 5: just start it on the rinse cycle. OK, let me do it for you, yes, you're welcome." Josh loved it!

The next problem turned out to be yet another missing sock: Josh thought there must be a Gremlin or Sock Fairy in his laundromat, who sneaks into washing machines every now and then to borrow socks: there can be no other explanation. This time though was different, the sock was found, jamming and breaking the pump shaft to impeller seal, and maybe, just maybe, that caused a frustrated foot to kick small contusions in the front panel of the machine: could have been. Josh really hated dealing with uptight people: he really hated it.

In the afternoon Josh got a reprieve by way of a grocery and produce order via satellite radio service, from the general store at Ambler. The owner of the store was a Vietnam Vet who flew groceries and other goods from either Anchorage or Fairbanks to Ambler, to keep his store stocked with whatever the villagers needed. Gerard's Cessna 180 was having problems again or he'd have picked up the stuff himself, as usual. His 180 probably had 15,000 hours on it by now. He should bury it and get a new one instead of repairing it, and repairing it, and keep repairing the repairs. He had more duct tape on that plane than paint: really, it was time to move on to newer flying hardware.

Josh drove the van into Fairbanks to Robert's, the local

produce wholesaler on College Rd. and from there on to the Northward Hub on lower Cushman to pick up the rest of the needed merchandise. What the Hub didn't have Josh picked up at Safeway at the University Mall before heading back to Goldstream Valley. The Hub was a so called Wholesaler and Safeway a retailer. The only real difference was that the Hub would pick the goods for you and if you bought enough, they'd deliver if asked. The prices were about the same in both places.

Josh was happy to fly most anything to Ambler because he resold the produce and other groceries, at a 50% markup for cash, and was then able to trade his flight time for high quality Jade that came from a fairly small Mountain of it just a very few miles north east of Ambler up the Kobuk River. Raw Jade was a small but steady summertime seller at the store and he did ship a few hundred pounds south from time to time. He even had some inquiries from China but nothing ever came of them.

First thing Monday morning he'd fly out to Ambler with the groceries and produce. He'd further fill the plane "to the gills" with soda pop since pop was a constant seller and you could never get enough of it to the villages in the bush.

Josh knew Dave, the Air Taxi Operator in Ambler. He almost always had a good supply of Jade that Josh could buy. If Dave was off making a buck, usually Gerard at the Ambler Store would have jade to trade. Instead of deadheading back to Fairbanks, it could be a moneymaking return.

Dave and Gerard had a running feud going. Gerard sometimes flew passengers into Ambler from Anchorage. Dave had the Air Taxi License and said Gerard was taking the food off his table. Gerard said, Dave should get a life and quit whining. They spoke on occasion but never did any business with each other. Josh was friendly with both Gerard and Dave and tried to get them to end their feud. Try as he would they never worked it out: they never even tried.

Ambler is a dry Village and Josh respects that. Some other

folks did not and they'd fly booze into any town that had the cash, even the dry bush Villages. Josh might deliver booze to a sandbar or most anywhere he could find a flat place land, but not if it was going to a dry Village. The Indians had enough problems: Josh felt he shouldn't add to their misery.

On Sunday Claire closed the store at 6:00 pm. Josh arrived from his grocery run minutes later and grabbed a bottle of wine as he walked thru the liquor store and climbed the stairs to their second floor apartment. Claire already had their steaks thawed and lit the briquettes while the "Master of Flight Operations" opened the bottle and poured: a Mondovi Merlot, life was good.

Monday morning started with the sound of a 206 taking off going south. The Grizzly Air Taxi Service operated out of Fairbanks International but their three planes, a Super Cub, a 180, and the 206 were generally parked just off the little strip behind the Ivory Exchange. During the winter when it snowed it was easier for the business owners to clean snow from the planes without having to drive to Fairbanks International and deal with locked gates and ground traffic control. There was also that monthly tie-down fee on the east ramp at Fairbanks International. Grizzly Air wanted to lease a hanger at International and probably would when one became available again. The pipe line boom caused a fairly long waiting list for covered space.

Of the six homes on the little airstrip behind the Exchange, two had hangers: big hangers. It was in Claire's long term business plan to buy one of these homes: the one with the largest hanger.

Grizzly employed pilots by contract, independent operators who got paid by the flight and paid their own Social Security and health insurance: they have no benefits at all, which was why they seem to feel no responsibility for the well being of the planes they fly. Contract pilots are notorious for being uncaring about their aircraft; some seem almost hostile and consider themselves in training and only want to gain flight hours as quickly as possible.

To add the precious numbers to their log books is the quest of a lot of the young, just starting, commercial pilots, and some if not most, develop a few pretty bad flight habits.

The pilot just now leaving in the Cessna 206 was most probably one of those just mentioned. He ran the prop up to 2700 RPM and kept it there till the plane was out of sight. It's OK to fly like that when necessary but for a mostly empty plane leaving an airstrip with a 400 ft elevation and a cool morning takeoff? It's just plain wrong! It wastes fuel and engine hours and really annoys the hell out of folks trying to sleep. Other than being a bit of a jerk, the pilot is insuring that he'll never fly for Josh, if another pilot is ever needed and hired.

Josh was in his front room on the top floor apartment still in his night clothes, lamenting the noise from the 206 takeoff, when a super Cub landed. He didn't recall seeing this plane before; maybe it was a very early customer, he hoped. The Cub taxied up next to the rear dock at the Ivory Exchange and idled for a minute before shutting down. As the pilot stepped out of the plane Josh remembered seeing him once before, nosing around behind the store about a week ago.

Angel stood between the store and the pilot, not about to give way to the visitor. This time he was dressed like a pilot and not an Ivory Exchange dinner guest. It was almost 6:30 in the AM, Claire was still in bed but Josh heard her getting up now and getting into the shower. He'd just put together a pot of coffee and was thinking of frying up a few eggs and bacon. The Ivory Exchange wouldn't be open till 11:00 for the lunch bunch, and Claire wouldn't open the store till 9:00. Josh walked out onto the balcony and said "Good Morning, want a cup of mud?"

"And good morning to you: yes I would love a cup, do I come up the back steps?"

"Yes, I'll leave the door open"

Angel sniffed the visitor and wagged a bit to let him by.

Josh put on his jeans and a tee shirt plus a pair of tennis shoes dressing for a run to Fairbanks to get the van serviced. The back door opened and Jim Littlejohn came through for a morning cup. Angel followed him in, looking for maybe a strip of bacon. Josh told Claire that she should be decently dressed as they had company for breakfast. Jim Littlejohn introduced himself, said he was a partner in a mining development firm from Fargo, North Dakota.

Jim and Josh talked a little about the delivery business that Josh had and about several mines in the area. Littlejohn said he visited Earl Pilgrim at the Stampede Mine, and that Earl had mentioned Josh and his small cargo delivery service: Earl always looked to help his friends. Jim had been inquiring to buy a lease on the Stampede mining operations, and Earl said he might think about it but probably couldn't lease the mine because, while the mine was presently idle, its operations were leased to a mining contractor in Seattle. Earl had "first refusal" for the lease, so he'd have to buy the lease back before selling it to Jim Littlejohn and Associates. Jim already knew this. Earl then said he might think about selling the claim acreage, buildings, and all equipment, and might give a twenty-five year lease on the existing Antimony, and other mineral rights, except for gold. Jim Littlejohn said he'd have to talk to his investors about it and would get back to Earl before the freeze up.

Littlejohn left after meeting Claire and said he might stop by the store to see the ivory inventory before returning to Fargo. He asked about the masks, the ones with rabbit fur surrounding the face. He thought they were made in Atigun Pass but Josh knew he meant Anaktuvuk Pass. Claire said they had three masks for sale but they were quite expensive.

Josh wondered why Jim Littlejohn was offering all this information to a stranger: curious! But it seemed interesting enough and finally, Josh knew something about new "goings on" that Skip maybe did not. Skip had mentioned some wise

50

guys from Fargo who seemed to have more money than brains: Josh wondered if Littlejohn was one of them.

Josh also wondered why anyone would want to mine Antimony again. As far as he knew, it was needed to harden the lead plates in storage batteries, and a small amount was used in linotype machines to harden news type. Neither of these businesses seemed to be expanding very fast.

Earl started his mining operations in the late 1920s but made most of his money during the war when submarines needed batteries and the Navy paid anything you asked to get Antimony. Earl had a high grading and concentrating operation at the mine. He had a whole purple mountain of the ore right in the middle of his claim, with some of it 50% pure.

With a large Caterpillar tractor he'd pull huge sledges of the concentrated mineral ore, "Stibnite", down the Toklat River to the Kantishna River, and then on to the Tanana River, and finally into the town of Nenana to the railroad. It was quite a long haul but had to be done when the rivers were frozen. The ore then shipped south on the Alaska Railroad. After some success he was able to build his own airstrip out of the mine tailings fairly close to his concentrators. The mineral prices were high enough then, to allow him to fly the mineral to the airstrip in Nenana in DC3s.

Today, nuclear powered Submarines and new printing techniques, along with other market forces, have pushed the demand for Antimony down to the point that production costs sometimes exceed sales, hence no profits.

The Stampede mining and milling operations now sit quietly, waiting for ore prices to rise. The buildings are slowly vegetating, and rotting away. Earl Pilgrim lives part time at the mine and part time in Fairbanks: he does the minimum yearly work to keep the claim valid but beyond that he enjoys the solitude of the Kantishna mining district and Stampede creek.

Hunters visit the airstrip in the fall, fishermen fly in for grayling, and tourists visit to photograph the mining facility in the summer months. Earl filed a gold mining claim in the fall of last year: he claimed it was to make a few bucks for his old age. It remains to be seen if the claim will be allowed as there is little gold to be found there.

Not slowed by his own questions, Josh was anxious to impress Skip with the new found gossip. As soon as the van was serviced, with a $75.00 oil change, Josh stopped in at The Gold Bar Exchange for lunch and to one-up Skip. But guess who was there talking to Skip: Jim Littlejohn!

# CHAPTER EIGHT

## — MORE QUESTIONS THAN ANSWERS —

JOSH SAID his "how does" to Skip, nodded to Jim, found a table, and ordered a Moose Burger with a side of potato salad. He overheard none of the conversation between Skip and Jim, but at one point it seemed to be getting a bit heated and Josh had his curiosity peaked. Jim left after a half an hour and a couple of beers: Skip was having his third Maker's Mark, neat. Wasn't it a bit early to be "half in the bag?"

Apparently Skip and Jim were old acquaintances, but not old friends. He and Skip had done business on and off for years. The dealings are always shady and close to the line, if not over it. Skip said Jim Littlejohn was more a con man and very much not a miner. Skip suggested that Josh look very carefully at any business dealings with him: "Get paid first or don't do it" was Skip's advice.

Skip also told Josh that somehow or another Jim might be involved or have an interest with the R&R deliveries to the Coleville River bar and for Josh to be careful, very careful. Josh didn't tell Skip about the extra and somewhat mysterious packages also delivered, and now he was glad he hadn't mentioned the new airstrip down river from the booze delivery site.

Finishing lunch, Josh headed back to the Valley. After checking in with Claire and putting the receipts in the cash register, he loaded the plane with the groceries and soda pop for tomorrow's delivery to Ambler: the produce was already bagged and in the store's only large cooler, the beer cooler, and ready to be put in the plane just before morning takeoff .

Suddenly, and a hell of lot faster than he should've been going, Pete drove around the store and pulled his car in next to the 185: he parked it under the wing and Josh was instantly pissed! He explained to Pete in spades that the parking lot in front of the store was the proper place to leave his car: "That's why it's called a parking lot."

Josh: "Move your damn vehicle right now."

It was not a request; it was a "do it or suffer".

Josh: "Don't ever drive your car in here like that and never get a car this close to my plane, never!"

After Pete moved his car, it took just a few minutes, he came walking back with a small package under his arm. Josh took a few minutes and calmed down a bit. He explained, he did not apologize, but related how a few years ago in Yakutat a car had brushed a chopper that he was responsible for and the repair bills for a door and landing skid came to over $3,000: the driver of the car was not only drunk but also uninsured.

Pete just held the package: he was a little pissed himself and was understandably less than cordial after being shouted at. Pete asked if Josh could deliver a package to the river bar and if so when: could it be soon?

Pete said "We'd pay $700.00 for the delivery if you can do it tomorrow."

This was really good luck since Josh would be returning from Ambler tomorrow and only have to fly a hundred miles out of his way to hit the gravel bar on the Coleville. This would be like free money and get him maybe a gold star from Claire.

Josh said, "I think I can be on the bar at 2:00 pm tomorrow, can you arrange for the pickup then? And, what the hell happened to that shot up flat bottom?"

Pete said he knew nothing of a riverboat, sarcastically like who gave a damn. But when Josh mentioned the blood, Pete got very interested and asked if Sam was OK. Josh asked who Sam was and Pete said he thought it was Sam's boat but other than that he knew really nothing of the incident.

Again, more questions than answers but there was little more to say. Just as Pete turned to leave, the frustration in Josh boiled up, and he said: "I will be happy to pass on this delivery, and future one's also. I haven't a clue what's going on but I don't like what I see. If this is some kind of weird game I'm not playing: get it? I have a business to run and this is getting spooky to say the least"

Pete: "You're a delivery service and a fairly good one, but beyond that it's none of your damn business."

Josh had trouble not going ballistic. Angel was standing alongside of Josh and moved in between him and Pete. She was just waiting for direction: she'd take Pete down in a Seattle minute if she got the word. Angel didn't know that seven years old was considered past her prime. Angel thought "Prime hell, I just want to bite the bastard."

Josh couldn't figure the little jerk out; he could've broken him in pieces and Pete knew it. Just the same Pete stood there nose to Adam's apple, so close that Angel was pushed away. Pete seemed unconcerned with his position: he was either really brave or really stupid: and that little bulge under his belt: it'd only get him in more trouble if push came to shove.

Then Pete backed down a little: he stepped back and said, "I've a bunch on my mind and I just want tomorrow's delivery to happen as scheduled. I'm sorry I said that, you're a trusted pilot and we appreciate your skill and the fact that what you say is what happens."

Josh said, "It will happen tomorrow on the river bar at 2:00 pm. When will I get paid?"

"On the gravel bar when the goods are delivered, I'm sorry I don't have the cash with me now, this wasn't planned for in advance: kind of spur of the moment."

Pete left for the parking lot, and Josh went upstairs to the apartment to lock up the package in his combination lock safe. Josh has it lag bolted to an interior wall filled with concrete. He stores his collection of twenty valuable antique firearms, mostly shot guns, in the safe also and seldom trades or sells these collectables but from time to time does add or subtract from the collection. He had to sell four old Greener shotguns to make the down payment on the store: it had been a tough decision but that was his decision, with no regrets.

Josh also has a key locking gun safe for his less valuable

but more practical guns. He took off his shoulder holster and 44 Magnum Revolver and locked them up. Then he walked next door to The Ivory Exchange for a drink and a pool game, to try to calm down a little. On his way across the parking lot he noticed a couple of cars, Hertz rentals that he'd seen at The Gold Bar and Lounge a couple of hours ago: Strange.

Tommy Wilson was ready for pool as always, but Josh was surprised to see Claire in a booth interviewing a young gal for a clerk's position. With their new found wealth from the whiskey deliveries she could afford to hire another clerk. Jean, Claire's present Head Clerk, was watching the store now, and would close up at 9:00 pm. If Jean had her way, and she always had her way, the store would close at exactly 9:00 pm: to the minute, which it did.

Josh wondered if tomorrow would be his last trip. He thought maybe he had been too forceful with Pete, maybe too much of a bully. He wanted the whiskey deliveries to continue because it was a great money maker and a really easy flight. He also liked the Coleville River, full as it was of Grayling and not fished all that much. In some ways the North Slope of the Brooks Range was like a different world: virgin and unspoiled except for Deadhorse and the Prudhoe Bay area.

Josh figured tomorrow would be interesting day because he intended to find out exactly what was going on. He really wanted to know what they were looking for at the strip mining site. He also thought he might throw his fly rod in the plane: just in case.

MORNING was wind calm with a little fog sitting in the low areas behind the store. After bacon and three eggs he grabbed his flight jacket and walked down the outside stairs to the back porch of the store. He almost forgot the produce and realized he was still a little uptight. Angel said her "how does " and got an ear scratch. Claire was behind the counter making change for some propane she had pumped and also selling laundromat tokens. She could do several things at one time: Josh knew he could never be as effective as Claire: she could keep track on a jobs list while answering the phone or even dealing with irate customers. Josh had bought a winning ticket in a Wife Lottery: for sure.

Josh was more a serial thinker and very good with complex problems, if not distracted. Josh had his way of doing things and, if not bothered with trivia, seldom missed the little details that Claire would think unimportant or not relevant to the task. They made a great team, had been one for a number of years.

When Josh was saying his "I will see you later", as usual, he left a written agenda and list of where and when he planned to be where ever. Claire put it on the cork board next to her inventory wish list.

The liquor salesman from P&J was due today. and probably hoped to write up another order for a pallet of R&R: after all he was on commission.

With Josh leaving, Angel jumped around like she wanted to go with him today and on a fluke, Josh said OK. It only took a few minutes to put the front seat back in and rearrange the soda pop. She would go on a few trips every now and then, but mainly stayed at the store with Claire. With Claire a passenger in the plane, Angel always went along. This time it was different but Josh said, "OK, kennel up in the plane." Angel rode in the front seat. She'd learned not to resist the seat harness and liked to look out the windows: Josh said, in a former life she was probably a Combat Pilot but for the wrong Air Force: hence her return as a dog. Angel had no clue where they were going but once there she always seemed to know the direction home.

From the Store to Ambler via Allakaket was about 300 nautical miles. From there to the Coleville River bar was another 125 miles, and back to Fairbanks International made a round trip of about 750 nautical miles. Even without reserve his range at economy cruise was not much more than 750 nm. Josh decided to top off at Allakaket on the way to Ambler. Fuel isn't available at Allakaket but Josh knew an Air Taxi operator there who'd sell him what he needed. That would give him an honest reserve for the round trip. If no fuel was available at Allakaket, Josh could still fly to Ambler and then to the Coleville River for the package delivery. He'd still have plenty of fuel to hit Bettles, where he could get lunch at the Sourdough Lodge at the airport and hopefully get gas from Kevin, his mechanic friend with a hanger in Bettles. The last time Josh was in Bettles, Kevin was out in the bush repairing a wing on a float plane. He wanted to see Kevin to find out if he knew anything about the new strip on the Coleville. Kevin was a good source of airplane gossip.

Then Josh could head back home to the store. It seemed it might be a long day but he'd not be lonely because he had Angel as a passenger.

On the trip to Allakaket, Angel slept, in spite of being held up in a clumsy way by the harness. She was snoring lightly as Josh hummed a country and western song that he thought was written by Willie Nelson, but stopped humming "Crazy" when he remembered Patsy Cline had made a big hit record of the song and then died in a plane crash. It might be bad Karma to sing about a plane crash while flying, Josh thought.

The ride was smooth: what a great day to be flying! Josh practiced letting the plane fly by its self and controlled his altitude only with throttle and his direction with rudder trim. He flew along for over half an hour without touching the yoke.

Landing in Allakaket, Josh found no one home at the Air Taxi Operation. He'd have to refuel at Bettles on his return trip according to his "plan B". Allakaket has about 100 people in town and only one general store, now managed and run by the Native Corporation, which bought out the original owners a few years ago: grocery prices went down and store profits went up. Good management will do that.

The stores present manager is a young Native guy with a pretty good handle on profit and loss. He willingly bought every can of pop Josh had in his plane and asked whether or not Josh was a potential buyer of Native handicrafts or raw furs that the store traded for groceries and other goods. The man wanted to wholesale the crafts but wasn't sure how to go about it. Josh promised to come back within two weeks with a craft buyer, Claire, who would be pleased to make the short flight if it gave her another source of Native art.

The flight leaving Allakaket was a little bumpy. Josh crossed the 4,000 ft. high foot hills approaching Ambler. Angel woke up and wanted to play: Josh wanted her back to sleep.

The Ambler River runs into the Kobuk River at the town of Ambler. There's a 3,000 foot runway with a smaller cross wind runway planned. The airstrip is unattended; no services are available. It's a little walk north of town. Josh flew low, 500 feet above the store, and exercised the prop, which was a standard signal to store keepers throughout the state that either a buyer or seller was arriving at the airport. By the time he over flew the runway to determine wind direction and landed, a young Native kid on a four wheeler pulling a small trailer was waiting for him. Most all the dogs in town were kept tied and the teenager told Josh that the few running loose were harmless, and Angel would be OK to wander around. Josh told Angel to stay close. She did: she was working this day, not playing.

The Ambler Store was owned and operated by one of the

only two white men in the village. He was well known but just tolerated by the town folks. An older Native man owns a part time store there, but he has trouble keeping it stocked because just about everyone in town steals from him. If you steal from the Ambler Store you're banned and not allowed back for three months. If you steal from the Native owned store: well it's not really stealing because most of the village folks are family, or at least cousins, and it's kind of OK to take what you need in the village culture.

The Native owned store, unable to keep much in the way of inventory, seldom has regular hours so it isn't much of a store. The owner has a really old Cessna 170 and flies once or twice a month to Anchorage or Fairbanks for inventory if he can scrape up some bucks. He had zero credit at Northward Hub because of unpaid billings. He's also rumored to be the supplier of booze in the dry town of Ambler.

For a small payment the boy told Josh he'd unload the plane and pull the groceries to the store. Josh gave him $5.00 and promised another $5.00 if he would pull 300 lbs of jade back to the plane later.

The kid said, "Yes I will, but please don't tell Gerard that you paid me. He might want part of it." Josh agreed but knew full well Gerard would never do that. He left the plane open and he and Angel walked to the store. By the time he got to it the boy was already there carrying the groceries and produce up the stairs. Gerard paid the invoice on the spot and asked if Josh wanted any jade. The price was the same as always and Josh gave him back some of bills he'd just been paid. Gerard and Josh shook hands and enjoyed a Pepsi on the porch while trading a few stories and talking about their Vietnam days, and how life was much better now.

Gerard's wife, Shelly, was in Montana for a few weeks with her folks, who were getting pretty old and needed either someone to work their Cattle Ranch or to sell it. Gerard told Josh he might be relocating to Montana if he could find a buyer for the Store: he asked Josh to spread the news that the Ambler store was for sale, and to please tell Skip Davis too. He thought Skip might know of a buyer. As Shelly was a Montana cow girl to begin with, Josh figured within the year Gerard would be gone. Gerard said, he might make a hell of a Cowboy if he could lose his fear of horses.

Josh said that he personally had no fear of horses but he had a real fear of horseshit.

The soda pop was drained and after turning down a lunch invitation, Josh was back at the plane loading the jade. No one else is allowed to load his plane: well maybe Claire. Josh gave the Native kid another $5.00 bill and then picked his spare sun glasses off the boy's face: the ones the kid must have found in the pilots side pocket in the cabin.

The boy said, "I guess I kind of forgot about those."

Josh gave him a couple of candy bars from his survival kit and said, "See you later."

Josh: "Angel, kennel up!"

And she jumped into the front seat and sat still while Josh put her harness on. Sure, the kid gets a candy bar and I get a harness: no justice today!

The trip from Ambler to the Coleville River bar was 175 miles with 6,000 ft high mountains to be crossed in the Brooks Range. Josh's initial heading was 33 degrees east of north, and after the first 100 miles it was all downhill at an oblique angle across the North Slope.

The North Slope, the famous North Slope, was not all that much different from the South Slope: Just a little more snow in the summer. But in the winter it was very different: the sun sets on the "Slope" a month after the Autumn Equinox and rises for the first time each year early April. In the winter months the Slope is as cold and dark and about as unfriendly a place as can be found.

During the summer the lower delta areas are vicious with insects that seem to be the main diet of the migrating water fowl who arrive shortly after the thaw and the first sunrise of the year. Still, a few Indian villages exist on the Slope. Many subsistence Eskimo villages are on the north and west coasts. Josh thought of himself as a pretty tough guy but knew his toughness was nothing compared to the Natives who lived in this harsh environment. He always had profound respect for the Natives of the north and tried to treat them decently and fairly. His one and only problem with Skip Davis was the man's treatment of Natives when he traded goods with them. When Skip did business he drove hard bargains whether dealing with Natives or White Folks alike. The White Folks in business were mostly able to handle him, but Skip took hard advantage of the Natives whenever he could.

Josh told an interesting story about an ivory trade he'd made in Browerville, a town next to Barrow, a little south of Point Barrow. Josh worked for a Scientist at the Geophysical Institute, U of A, Fairbanks, one spring for a month and a half while his airplane engine got rebuilt. Josh  assisted, just doing the grunt work, for Ice Stress Studies on  the Shore Fast Ice. The work involved drilling ice cores, freezing in a few flat jacks, and running a front loader to push around snow and to pull piping out of the Shore Fast Ice. Josh stayed at the Navel Arctic Research Laboratory, a facility administered by the University. The Lab was just east of town and a little too far to walk. So he "borrowed" a vehicle from the Lab one night and drove into Browerville to find  ivory Christmas gifts for Claire and his Mom. He'd heard that a "Whaling Captain", Harry Brower, had a few pieces of local native art for sale. After getting very confusing directions from several groups of Native folks, Josh finally found Harry Brower's home.

It turns out that giving directions is a learned skill. In a very small town most everyone knows most everyone, where they live, and how to get there. No one really ever needs to give direction so the people have never developed the skill to give or take directions. Now because of things like this, Skip

Davis and folks like him might say the Native folks are stupid, when in fact the ability to give directions is a learned trait and has little to do with intelligence.

When Josh finally found the Brower home he walked to the front door and knocked on it. Nothing happened: he knocked again, still nothing. Then a couple of kids walked in and a few more walked out. As one young boy came out he asked Josh what he wanted and indicated he should go inside to find "The Captain". Josh did and found an older woman who said, "Harry is in the garage in back of the house with his crew."

Josh walked around back and saw a garage-shop kind of building with a couple of Eskimos smoking Pot and two others smearing what seemed to be grease on the inside ribs of a boat.

The whale boat in the building was ancient but absolutely perfect: maybe twenty-two feet long, wooden rib construction, and tightly covered with walrus skin. The ribs of the boat weren't screwed together but were held fast with shoe laces, which turned out to be strips of Caribou hide. There was a Super 10 hp Mercury outboard motor from the 1950s mounted on the back, and a one inch bore brass cannon mounted in the front from the late 1800s. Josh wished then and still wishes, he'd had a camera with him because few could believe what a perfect piece of whaling equipment he'd seen.

After a clumsy intro, Josh asked, "How's the whaling going?"

Harry Brower said, "Eskimos three, Whales one" and winked."

Josh didn't know if that was true or not: turns out it was. Josh asked about ivory and Harry went into the house and came out a few minutes later with really nice pieces. After a little bargaining Josh bought the lot of them and was thrilled. A few years later, when Josh was better informed about ivory, he discovered Harry Brower had resold him elephant ivory. Harry made regular ivory purchases from Hong Kong by mail, just for the tourists who came to Point Barrow in summer.

Trip time to the Coleville was about 1:20 minutes. His fuel supply was as planned, and he felt pretty good about the flight. The sun was at his back and he wished for an autopilot: if he ever got a 206 it would be his first "goodie". Angel was getting damn tired of the harness but knew Josh wouldn't release her from her bondage until they were on the ground. On this leg of the trip, as a joke, Josh put earmuffs on her and a scarf around her head to hold the muffs. She didn't like all that on her head but she did seem to enjoy the quiet. "At least my nose still works."

## CHAPTER TEN

### — A Few Answers, A Package to Colville —

JOSH DECIDED to overfly the camp and buildings that looked like a strip mining operation, that he'd seen two days ago. He figured Carter was there and wanted him to know Josh was aware of the facility. Then Josh headed back the 20 miles up the Colville and landed on the gravel bar in the middle of the river. The flow was pretty strong and the bar getting smaller by the day. He'd arrived early and decided to fly fish again until the pickup boat came. Angel was happy to run around some and roll in what was left of a dead salmon. She was told to stay away from the small willow and Josh showed her the half burned hornets' nest. Angel saw no bees of any kind but could still smell the gasoline burned the nest: Angel doesn't like gas or bees but she really likes to roll on dead salmon.

Josh had a wet fly on and was drifting it along the bottom when he hit his first fish. Angel tried to help him land it but Josh told her to "sit, stay, and get the hell out of the water."

Angel thought, "What a grump!"

A sixteen inch Brown trout was not unheard of but was very unusual. Josh was thrilled: he normally caught Grayling and an occasional Rainbow trout.

Josh had his second fish on when they heard the jet boat coming up stream: he cranked in his fourth Grayling and had it on the stringer with two Browns just as the jet boat pulled up on the bar.

The larger of the Indians, who had worked the previous pickup, piloted the boat, with Carter Thomas in it. The Indian looked bigger this time for some reason. Darker clothes maybe.

Carter took the package and opened it but didn't let Josh see what was in it. He paid Josh the $700.00 and thanked him: crisp new hundred dollar bills again. He asked Josh what he had talked to Jim Littlejohn about.

Josh said, "How do you know I talked to Littlejohn? It's

really not your concern who I talk to or what we talk about"

Carter: "Did you tell him anything about the landing strip or the facility that you just flew over down river?"

Josh: "My conversations with Mr. Littlejohn are not your concern: they're private as are most all my conversations, but no: I did not speak to him about anything concerning deliveries to you or anything about you or your facilities. He is not aware that I make deliveries to you, our discussions did not include my work for you in any way."

Carter: "Jim Littlejohn is very aware that you make whiskey deliveries to us. He somehow thinks that the whiskey distribution network on the North Slope is his franchise and only his: you will probably be hearing from him. He thinks he's a dangerous man, loves to give orders, and thinks he must be obeyed when he speaks. He really is just a cheap hood: but he may still be quite dangerous."

Carter explained that he and Littlejohn were competitors and Josh should be aware, Jim's not the good guy he pretends to be, and Josh might have to decide which side he was on, and that the whiskey business would be gone by choosing unwisely.

He said it nicely but it also kind of sounded like a threat: Josh studied Carter's eyes and gathered no understanding of what was happening, so Josh didn't respond at first. He'd lost tract of the big Indian but was not surprised to find Angel with her tail down, a few feet behind him, between him and The Indian. Josh figured it was time, he decided to go for it.,

Josh said "What exactly is going on at that strip mine? Why have I been flying booze in here and being paid twice what you'd have to pay other pilots to do the same? And why is Littlejohn trying to lease a mine at Stampede Creek that has no value? What does he have to do with anything? Give me some real answers and make me believe what I'm doing is legal or I am gone!"

After some thought Carter said "Ok, what the hell, I can tell you this much."

Carter said that some of the booze was just a little gift/payment/bribery on top of the large payments to get his equipment quietly trucked up the Haul road. Besides paying the drivers well for transporting the equipment that Josh had seen at the "Strip mine", which was no "strip mine", Carter had been doling out the whiskey to the drivers as a thank you to hush it up. The rest of it went for resale in Deadhorse to pipe line workers.

Carter said, "These drivers will work real hard and keep quiet about it if they think it's illegal. The booze, it's a gift, but it'll go away if the word gets out: and these guys like gifts." $200 in booze is worth $2,000 in hush money in this business. The equipment that you saw at the new air strip was mostly hauled up the old Taps Road, the Ice Road, by the same trucks and truckers who now haul to Deadhorse at Prudhoe Bay. That route is closed to us because of environmental and political concerns."

Carter said, he now had a guy at the Terminal in Fairbanks and what he needs for mining at his facility is loaded last and comes off first, at a staging facility on the haul road that's after Atigun Pass but before Galbraith Lake.

"We'll pull it over here after freeze up on an old trail. Everything you see there now, at the airstrip, was trucked up the Taps Road or pulled over last winter on the old sled road by two Cat tractors, one of which you saw at the site. It took four trips across the old sled road in the dead of winter to get the building materials here. We'll have to start flying fuel in pretty soon. We were flying in groceries and other stuff but our pilot had bad luck and flew into a mountain in bad weather. We mostly get our groceries now in Deadhorse quite legally. We can't get our whiskey through Deadhorse, it's a dry town and Alyeska has been checking the loads."

Carter went on: "That's why we need the Golden Valley Store and the Goldstream Aviation Services. You've a retail license and can legally deliver anywhere in the state, I think.

We started you slow and watched to see if you said what you would do and then did what you said. You've been spot on: we like that! Now that you know this you're part of it, the flying business will continue if you want it to and it'll be profitable, but understand this: if you open your mouth about our facility you'll lose our business and be in more trouble than you can imagine. This is not a threat but please understand we are in a very serious business, and you did ask. We think, because you work for us, at least a little, you've a moral obligation not to spread information about our business to those not associated with our interests: don't you agree?"

Josh was surprised to say the least, and although he nearly hit his flashpoint with the non-threat, he calmed a little and decided to not respond. He needed the money he made from the booze deliveries; he didn't want the business to stop just yet. He asked "Why don't you fly the booze to Umiat and bring it to the strip mining site in boats?"

Carter said, "We did that once but almost all of it was stolen and too many people were beginning to nose around our operation: we tried several times. Hector is happy with the setup now and he does his thing very well. If he's happy, we're happy. Deadhorse is dry for a very good reason: and stop calling it a strip mine, it is not a strip mine!"

"Well, what the hell is it?" Josh said

Carter said "For now it's not your concern, if you don't know you can't tell. Your concern is whiskey and a few other strategic deliveries. Future deliveries should be to the new air strip down river, but you're asked to fly first to Ambler, or some other out of the way place, as you did today. Just land for a while and look around to make sure you aren't being followed. Then fly to the new facility and try to keep a low profile. We know it's a long way and if you can't fly safely due to weather or an incident, just abort the delivery for that day. If you must abort a delivery, fly back home you'll be paid for your flying time at ninety bucks an hour plus fuel, for your time in the air.

I know that much hardly covers your overhead but it might keep you from doing dumb by flying into marginal weather and killing yourself for a few bucks."

Josh asked him how he knew he was in Ambler today and Carter said he knew quite a bit, and just smiled.

Josh asked about Pete's role in this expanding mystery. Carter said Pete was a minor partner, but more than just an expeditor. He said Pete was a fairly bright guy in spite of his appearance and manner.

Carter said, "Pete knows no more about the operation than you do. If things work out as planned you and Claire will end up with a small part, a very small part of the business"

At first the dialog had been strained but as the tone of the conversation calmed down Angel was more at ease and now enjoying ear scratches from the big Indian. He seemed nice enough but smelled a little like the folks back in the Goldstream Valley.

It's been a long day for me and I'm getting hungry, Angel thought. She hoped Josh had another candy bar or something in his black bag in the plane. She walked to the river and got a drink. River water is good, now back to that dead fish.

## CHAPTER ELEVEN

### — BACK TO THE VALLEY, ALMOST —

THE JET BOAT LEFT the bar heading downstream: Josh felt a little tense but better: he finally had answers but was so full of information he had to digest it a bit before starting his flight home. He still had to fuel up in Bettles and get some lunch. He might also try to find a supplier of "Squaw Candy": Smoked Salmon Belly strips that so many folks in the Goldstream Valley had asked for. The Borough Health Inspector did not allow the sale of anything not produced and labeled according to the FDA particular set of rules: whatever the rules were. Smoked Salmon Bellies were on the list of items not allowed but neither Claire nor Josh gave a flying Hoot what the Health Inspector thought.

Angel seemed happy that just the two of them were alone on the bar: the conversation had been a little tense for her too, because she was the entire security patrol on this     mission, and she took her job seriously. Angel rolled on the     decaying salmon again and was happy that Josh had relaxed. Then Josh called her to the river bank and she knew she was about to get a bath. Josh didn't understand how nice she smelled after rolling around on a dead salmon: no one ever did.

Josh finally pacified Angel with a candy bar, when he tried to dry her. She really loved candy bars. She once found a supply of candy bars in the store and was perplexed when told that she couldn't help herself: it was her store too you know. Claire had given her a swat and that made her very sad. Angel didn't like swats, but that time it was almost worth it. And, it had been fun for a while: though she felt kind of sick after eating about six Snicker bars.

Josh was still a little preoccupied while preflighting the 185. He knew that the fuel supply was OK and the oil was only a half quart low. Brakes were solid, the flaps were OK, and all controls were free. The doors were locked and the harnesses

70

were secure on both Angel and him: the magnetos were good as always. Josh put in ten degrees of flap and pushed the prop and mixture controls to the wall. Then he pushed the throttle forward slowly trying to avoid pulling sand and gravel up from the bar into the prop.

They were off the bar in less than 600 feet. Josh thought he felt something a little sticky and mushy on takeoff, just before they left the ground, he needed some left rudder, like he was in mud or something. Everything else seemed OK, so he put it out of his mind and reached over and scratched Angel's ears. Angel thought: "I just got a candy bar, and an ear scratch: and now we are going home, Life is great!"

Josh set a course of 160 degrees magnetic and very slowly started his climb to 7500 feet to clear the highest peaks on his route. He set the prop to 2300 and manifold pressure at 23 inches. It was about 140 miles to Bettles and the highest peaks were in the first 70 miles. Josh dialed in the Bettles VOR frequency of 116.0 and would simply fly the needle, when he picked it up, after clearing the north/south divide of the Brooks Range.

The strip at Bettles is 5200 feet long. The pattern altitude is 1700 feet and there's usually a supply of 100 octane low lead fuel. He'd be there in an hour and ten minutes and was getting a hungry for a burger and soggy fries at the Old Sourdough Lodge, the only eatery in town: if it wasn't open, he only had candy bars and V8 juice: Angel hated V8.

Josh had to fly a little further east to enter a left base for runway 19. He dialed up 122.9 fifteen miles out and listened for traffic; he announced his landing five miles out and then switched frequencies to talk to Flight Services in Fairbanks on 122.2 to announce his arrival. He flew a left base to enter the pattern for runway 19: Flight Services doesn't really like "straight in landings."

Angel was asleep again but not snoring this time. Josh would've taken 40 winks too if he had an auto pilot: maybe when he gets a 206. When he could make out the Koyukuk River that runs just past the west side of Bettles, he did his radio work. He'd been cleared to land runway 19 thru the FFS in Fairbanks. With light variable wind, temp, humidity, and dew point. It all looked good to him

Josh made the last turn to the left and dropped the flaps to 30 degrees. He was on short final at about 70 knots, coming down slowly, and bleeding off a few knots. He'd touch down at about 50 knots with his fairly light load of dog and jade. Josh always tried to land three points or maybe tail first. He'd first flown a Cessna 170 and learned to land like that. The 185 did not have the good forward visibility of a 170 but it was OK as Josh sat high and the side vision was good.

A few more minutes and Josh and his loyal companion Angel, would be landing at the Bettles Airport, the gateway to the Bettles-Evansville thriving metropolitan area of 45 people.

First the tail and almost at the same time the Main gear touched down, and it seemed like a good smooth landing.

But then suddenly the landing was more like a ski run filled with "Moguls". The plane pulled hard to the right and started to dip the wing and try to spin out. Josh was full on the left brake and the 20 inch Tundra tire screeched and dug for traction. As the nose dipped Josh pulled full back on the yoke and went to takeoff power for a second or two until the prop wash pushed the tail back down. When the plane finally did come to rest his precious 185 was off the runway in the grass on what was a ski strip in the winter months. The 185 was at a strange angle and looked funny with only one tire and wheel. One shoe off, one shoe on, diddle diddle dumpling my son John.

Josh knew without even looking that he'd felt the right main tire go flat on takeoff from the bar and failed to recognize the problem at the time: poor form! If he'd known for sure the tire was destroyed on takeoff, he'd have landed on the grass strip that he now was parked on.

No one was more surprised than Josh, except Angel. She woke up and wanted out: It's a hell of a way to land and I want free of this damn harness. Josh got out his door and by the time he got around to the right side door, Angel was out of her harness, ready to "deplane". She jumped and ran around the plane twice growling and looking for someone or something to tear up. She was angry, pissed off and fearless: then and there Josh knew for sure that Angel would never back down from trouble, except if it involved a blue parrot.

He said "Good dog Angel!"

The almost famous part time Bettles Aircraft Mechanic and part time Air Taxi Operator, Kevin Ferguson, nephew of the also almost famous Bush Pilot Archie Ferguson, just happened to be standing beside his hanger smoking. He'd seen the whole incident and was impressed. He arrived on a four wheeler in less than two minutes and after a walk around the plane, asked Josh: "Would you care to purchase a new tire and wheel at 50% above retail, and what might you want me to do regarding the broken off runway light that is tangled up in your twisted brake line?"

Josh heard no part of the smart ass question. He was busy on the radio talking to Flight Services stating that he was now off the active runway: he failed to mention the part about his one wheeled 185 or the uneven number of lights on the right hand side of runway 19. He made a silent wish that no one else would either.

Kevin and Josh were old friends. They'd known each other from the helicopter flying gig that Josh did in Yakutat a few years back. Kevin worked as a chopper mechanic there, as well as a part time pilot. They'd both flown copters in the Vietnam thingy that was called a war. They were part of the only good thing that the war produced: a bunch of pretty good flyers: those that were left.

Angel was having none of this old friends crap. During the somewhat controlled crash she'd been clobbered by a hunk of jade: her back leg hurt. "Where's food? I want to go home!"

Kevin said, "A pilot out of Nome ordered a pair of ten inch wheels and they somehow got shipped here. Since he never picked them up, and I have them in inventory, if you want to buy the wheels, I'll take 15% as a commission and send the owner of the wheels the remainder of the money"

He continued, "I think the brake line, brake caliper, axel bearings, and other parts can be cannibalized from that wrecked 180 over there next to the hanger. It got wrecked on takeoff last month."

He also said "I've a couple of tires here but they're not 20 inch tundra tires, they are 850 by 10s: I have no idea how to get tundra tires quickly, it'll take maybe a week to get a pair."

The $550 price was staggering as were most things aircraft related.

Josh said, "Ok, go for it, I can do without tundra tires for the rest of the season: sand bars just cause trouble anyway."

Kevin thought he could repair the damage by tomorrow.

"Do you want to spend the night with us in the cabin?  I can call Molly and tell her we'll have visitors for the night."

"I guess so, and thank you"

Josh asked to help with the repairs. What he really wanted was to see that the work was done right.

Kevin said, "You can hand me tools but beyond that if I have your help it might take an extra day for the fix. Could you be a little more careful landing next time? By the way, my rate is $80 per hour, $85 for credit cards: And, guess what, I have a new credit card reader that I've yet to use"

Josh: "I am so very happy for you"

Kevin drove Josh back to the hanger and they got a small garden tractor and a three wheel dolly for transport. Back at the plane The dolly had a folding ramp and with both men pushing they got the bent and twisted wheel up on it. Kevin strapped it down.

Kevin: "What do you have in the plane, rocks?"

74

Josh: "A few hundred pounds of jade is all, want to buy a little? For you, a 15% discount"

Josh pulled the tongue of the dolly with the tractor and Kevin pulled the tail wheel of the 185 with the 4 wheeler. It took a coordinated pull but they had the plane back to Kevin's hanger without further damage and better than that, probably unnoticed. Josh looked around and decided since there had been no traffic or other witnesses he would do the FAA a really big favor and save them a whole bunch of paper work. He decided not to inform them of the incident. One less runway light was no problem and he ensured that the electrical leads to the light weren't shorted or exposed: what a good guy!

It was late in the day when Josh radioed Flight Services and asked them to relay a message to Claire.

Josh said, "Please tell her we're weathered in at Bettles and should be home by noon tomorrow."

The Flight Service Specialist at FAA said, "There are no reported weather problems in Bettles".

Josh said, "My bad, without thinking I had a beer with a friend and I don't want to fly after drinking".

The Specialist said, "It is a violation of FAA regulation 91.17 to fly within 8 hours of consuming alcoholic beverages."

Josh grabbed a pencil to quickly write that number down so he could hang it on the refrigerator. What a guy! He really knows the rules.

Dinner was salmon fillets and moose back strap steaks. It is referred to locally as "River and Swamp" by the few mostly ill bred residents of the area. Pretty much anything that can be consumed and that does not come out of a grocery store has a silly name. It's not just to save money; folks in the Bettles-Evansville area like to live independently. Almost everyone has a garden, if they've been in Bettles for very long. They hunt and fish too: why else would anyone be here?

Molly said she knew of a source of Squaw Candy from the tribe at Rampart. They intended to wholesale Salmon Belly strips last year but got so much crap from the commercial food watch dogs, they decided to just sell the stuff like they always did. Molly gave Josh the contact information. He thought maybe he would stop in Rampart on his way back to the Valley. Molly thought this time of year most of the able folks would be tending the fish wheels and the strips wouldn't be dried and smoked until later in the year. She suggested Josh go up there in August when there'd be many pounds of Squaw Candy available. She admonished Josh to not say Squaw Candy but instead to call it salmon belly strips. The tribes are sensitive about the word "Squaw".

## CHAPTER TWELVE

### — HOME AGAIN, LITTLEJOHN PROBLEMS —

REPAIRS ON THE 185 took less time than Kevin thought. Josh had been a help and because of that Kevin reduced his hourly rate to $79.50. The Log book still was a problem because the parts replaced made the accident obvious. Josh was reluctant to admit to the FAA that he had "a bit of a problem landing": Technically it was a crash landing, but it had happened, it was fixed, and it was over! Kevin didn't like it but finally signed off on the crash in the Airframe log book as routine maintenance, and a tire replacement.

With the smaller tires the plane sat lower on the ground. Better visibility when taxiing is always good. After a ground run up to check the brakes, and listening to Angel whining while being put in her seat harness, they were ready to go. Angel really didn't like the harness and wasn't all that crazy about getting back in the plane either. Josh bought 20 gallons of fuel which was half of the total supply available. He added a quart of oil and paid for it in spite of the fact he had several quarts in the plane already.

As Josh did the last of the pre-flight he saw a Super Cub landing and was pretty sure it was the same plane that Jim Littlejohn had flown into the strip behind the store. Josh didn't remember the Tail Number though. He told Kevin that the guy in the Cub might not be kosher and repeated the warning he'd gotten from Skip. Kevin also knew Skip, almost everyone did and that Skip was forthright with his friends. Kevin told Josh he'd keep his eye on Littlejohn.

With that Josh climbed into the 185, scratched Angel's ears, and started the engine. He planned on going to Fairbanks International for fuel before heading to the store. The takeoff was different than usual because of the smaller tires. The Cessna lifted from a three point attitude so perfectly, that Josh wasn't sure exactly when the plane left the ground: it was so smooth! It reminded Josh again of a profound observation made by a less than famous, but still one of the best bush pilots he'd ever flown with: Horace Black. Yes, most airplanes fly pretty well if the pilots don't screw up. He said it in a friendly way. He meant that Josh was over controlling his plane. Horace, the instructor, thought that Josh should just trim it out and let it fly by its self.

The flight back to Fairbanks was quicker than usual. The smaller tires had much less drag than the tundra size, and Josh picked up another six knots at cruise power. He set a course of 130 degrees. At 135 knots he'd cover the distance to Fairbanks in a little over an hour, depending on winds. Josh let the 185 go to 4500 feet before trimming out. The highest hills were 3200 feet: there were no clouds and it was CAVU. He let down a little going by the Yukon River Bridge and he circled very low over the mining operation of Ralph Sims at Livengood to say Hi. Back up to 2500 ft he could see Wickersham Dome on the horizon on his left and a little further Murphy Dome to the right.

Passing Murphy Dome he dialed his radio up to 118.3 and pushed the mike button on the yoke.

"Fairbanks Tower: this Cessna 99240 Alpha."

He heard: "Cessna 99240 Alpha go ahead."

Josh keyed in: "Cessna 99240 Alpha is six miles out over Ester Dome, in bound landing with information Sierra, request left base for Runway 1 left."

Tower replied, "Rodger 40 Alpha, enter left base for Runway 1 left: report over Tanana river."

Josh replied: "Left base for 1 left, report over the river: 40 Alpha."

When Josh crossed the Tanana River he keyed: "Tower, 40 Alpha is over the river turning on long final."

He heard: "Cessna 40 Alpha cleared to land, exit at mid field if able."

"Roger tower, right turn at mid field: 40 Alpha."

At mid field Josh turned off right and said "Tower, 40 Alpha is off the active runway."

He heard: "Cessna 40 Alpha contact ground on 121.9."

Josh said, "Fairbanks Ground: Cessna 40 Alpha is on taxi way Bravo: taxi for fuel."

Josh heard: "40 Alpha, taxi and hold short of Runway 1 right."

He said: "Hold short of 1 right: 40 Alpha"

As Josh neared runway 1 right, he heard: "Cessna 40 Alpha cross runway 1 right and taxi to ramp."

Josh taxied to Northwinds Aviation for fuel. When he stopped Angel wanted to get out but she knew she had to stay in the plane because she wasn't allowed on the ramp without a leash: tough to be a dog on a leash, even a good dog.

With the fuel pumped, Josh taxied to the runway and, having done the necessary radio work, took off south on 19 left, slightly down wind. He stayed low and was cleared to turn right for the short trip to Goldstream Valley.

Angel was finally able to get out of the plane after the landing at the store. She visited one of her favorite bushes to mark the south end of her boundary. She pretended to guard the jade as Josh tied down the vehicle that had almost killed her, landing in Bettles. Angel was no longer sure that the plane was her friend.

In the early afternoon, while the store's most senior clerk, Jean, had a bathroom break, Josh tended the register. In ten minutes he rang up bread, a case of Coke, a case of Miller, a liter of Gippo Vodka, and 18 gallons of gas. He got the great news that washer #1 wouldn't pump out the rinse water again. More socks, he thought: Wow, how do real folks handle the jammed sock in the pump problem? Do they call a repair man every time? I don't really think clean clothes are that important in the overall scheme of things, not at all.

When Jean returned to the cash register, Josh grabbed his tool box and headed across the parking lot to Soapies for the washer repair. Not a jammed sock, a frayed drive belt this time. He replaced it quickly and gave the lady with the soggy load of laundry two tokens. She was so happy she almost kissed him: Wonder what I could get for three tokens?

After the washer fix, Josh found the wheel barrow and unloaded the jade. He put it in the back room in Soapies where he stored salt for the softener and twenty bags of dog food: his backup supply, and one of Angel's favorite spots.

He'd have no problem finding a buyer for the 300 pounds of jade, all of it, at $19 per pound for the good stuff, less for the smaller pieces; he paid $3.50 per, but of course he had to fly it from Ambler: that wasn't a cheap trip.

Josh heard loud talking getting louder: he left his jade stacking chore and went out back to see what the noise was all about. Jim Littlejohn and a younger man had just landed and taxied up behind the Ivory Exchange, parking fairly close to the 185. They came in the Super Cub that Josh had seen in Bettles. Josh wondered if he had been followed: he thought probably yes, he wondered why.

There seemed to be an argument going on between Jim and Claire: it was heated. Josh stepped up, got between them, and tried trying to calm the conversation.

Claire: "I can handle this, JJ. I don't need help"

Jim, facing Josh, said "The liquor business on the North Slope is ours, you will stop your liquor deliveries now: it is my territory, not yours. I have the franchise for the Slope and you are interfering with our business plan. You will not be flying any more whiskey north unless or until you are working for me. Do you get it junior?"

Josh: "I've no idea what you are talking about, what franchise?"

Jim: "I have the franchise, the Fargo Cartel sold me the franchise, and I intend to protect it"

Josh: "What the hell is the Fargo Cartel"

Jim: "You keep flying whiskey north and you will damn

80

well find out what the Cartel is."

Josh: "I'll fly whiskey anywhere I damn well feel like it. You don't even have a liquor license, do you? You aren't even legal, are you? Who the hell do you think you are? Don't answer that, just get the fuck out of here, right now!"

The young guy, David Littlejohn, now argued with Claire, getting in her face. Claire also suggested in an unkindly way for them to leave the property, or get throw off. The young guy took a step toward Claire. Nose to nose with him, she didn't back down.

Claire: "You are not welcome here: you may leave now or get thrown out in 30 seconds!"

The kid put his hands on Claire's shoulders and pushed. She stood rock solid and he only managed to push himself backwards about a foot. Now he was really frustrated, and embarrassed in front of his father. He hauled back to take a swing at Claire and Angel took him down.

Angel had been waiting: she jumped at him from the side, putting her full momentum on his upper body. He hit the ground hard. Angel grabbed his arm and backed hard away from Claire. Stretched out, with his arm in the mouth of a 78 pound pissed off German shepherd, unable to reach his weapon, David Littlejohn was helpless.

Angel was well trained, having worked in the K9 unit of the Seattle Police department. She knew her job was to protect Claire and she did just that. Being well trained, she didn't go for the throat and try to kill or injure. Her job was to control and subdue. This she did very well.

The young guy on the ground was screaming and actually crying, when Josh sternly said, "Angel Cut!" Angel let loose of the arm but didn't back off. Claire quickly reached down and took the Glock from his belt holster. Angel growled and bared her teeth, 18 inches from the young guy's face who was now wetting his pants and crying out for help. Josh figured it out, that the young guy was Jim Littlejohn's son. Jim grabbed up a rake leaning by the loading dock of the Ivory Exchange. With it up, he moved toward Angel.

Claire said: "Back off! Put down that rake. Pick up that little prick, and get the hell out of here." She pointed the Kid's gun at him, without real thoughts of shooting.

Littlejohn said, "I'm going to kill that damn dog".

"You are like hell."

Swinging the rake he took a step forward. Before Angel could respond, Claire hammered his hand with the butt end of the kid's Glock. Littlejohn dropped the rake with a yelp and reached for his own side arm. Claire hit him with a roundhouse left hook. Jim littlejohn went down with a thud, on top of the rake, which produced yet another yelp. Jim Littlejohn really was having a real bad day.

Claire isn't a large woman yet she's hardly petite. She is tall, almost 5' 9" and 140 pounds, and has the body of a runner. In some of their more romantic, playful moments Josh and Claire had wrestled a little. Josh was surprised by her strength, but didn't think of her as a fighter. He'd never witnessed her being this aggressive. He was impressed!

Littlejohn rolled off the rake and sat on the ground slowly shaking his head. He responded to Claire's punch with threats of a law suit and promised: "This is not over, I will get you and your flyboy husband, this is not over."

Claire said, "Get you, your kid, and your god damn plane off of this air strip, or I will burn it where it sits. You return and there'll be more trouble than you can handle."

Josh: "Get yourself together guys. I suggest you fly away quickly. Don't even think about coming back. If you do, she might really get angry."

Claire: "Thanks for all the help, Josh"

Josh: "You said you had it covered. I did tell Angel to Cut."

Josh waited for the Littlejohns to pick themselves up; Claire called Angel, turned, and walked away. After pulling the tail of the Cub around, Jim and his son got back in the plane, not gracefully, ready to exit, but first, from inside the Super Cub, he yelled: "I will sue your business for everything you have, everything!"

"They can sue if they want to, but their law suit will not stand. I will see to that personally," said Don Peters, husband of Tommy Wilson, and half owner of the restaurant. He was also a retired Seattle Attorney.

Don had heard the commotion and stood ready to join the fracas, but it seemed he wasn't needed. Don was thinking that Tommy spent some time looking out for Claire, when Josh was away on a delivery trip. He wondered if it was backward, if maybe Claire should be watching out for Tommy, which seemed a bit more appropriate.

Josh got the finger from the kid on takeoff. Josh just stood there not quite knowing what to do. Nobody was going to tell him how to run his business and he'd never heard of the Fargo Cartel. But what the hell did just happen? He was not totally sure except he always knew not to get crossways with Claire. Maybe Jim Littlejohn now knew that also. Josh watched them fly south, probably back to International. Josh turned and walked to the back steps and climbed them to the apartment.

CLAIRE WAS FUMING: she was drinking, not sipping, a pretty big glass filled with ice cubes and Black Jack Daniels Tennessee sipping whiskey. She also had an iced dish rag folded over her left hand. It probably wasn't broken but she was left handed and she thought she'd probably need it now and then. Only Angel seemed to be content and calm. The bad guys were gone and Claire was OK, where was dinner?

Josh came thru the door and saw Claire.

"My hand is maybe broken, thanks for asking, and how was your day?"

Josh said, "My day was just fine except for a minor crash at Bettles, but that was yesterday. Did Flight Services get you the message?"

Claire: "I thought it was something like that, is the plane OK? You flew it back so it can't be too bad. What happened? Flight Services said you were in Bettles too drunk to fly. They asked if you tended to drink a lot, and how often? I told them you never drink within eight feet of a plane. They did not laugh. God, those guys are serious, why don't they get a life, at least maybe a little?"

Josh said, "The plane is fine but I had to buy a brake line, new wheels and new tires. Afraid it ate up the profit from the Ambler run. Kevin and Molly say Hi. I stayed with them and I owe Kevin big, really big, for the down low on the repairs. Claire, if anyone asks, the Ambler trip was routine, nothing happened in Bettles, except a tire change. By the way I will be making future deliveries to the new airstrip I told you about. I won't need Tundra tires for that and the new airstrip is, well, it should not come up in any conversation around here. We should be like Shultz: We know nothing! What the hell happened with that jerk you decked?"

Claire: "It started yesterday. Skip came to the Exchange

late afternoon and told Tommy about a young guy from Fargo, North Dakota, who asked about you at the Gold Bar. He knew more about our liquor sales than I do. He said we, both of us, the fabulous we, were involved with some drug and liquor running operations on the Colville River. Is that true? I thought we were just selling R&R to some truckers in Deadhorse. And what's this about drugs: we don't do drugs, right? He said it was his territory and he told Skip that you were to work for him or get out of operation, or else!"

Josh: "He can tell Skip whatever he wants. We don't do drugs, nothing involving drugs. I promise you that, we don't sell drugs. But we damn well sell liquor to any legal and willing buyer who steps up with the cash, any one! Fargo Cartel be damned. What the hell is the Fargo Cartel? These whiskey delivery flights are making us a good bucks, its good business. We are not leaving this profitable market, we are staying."

Claire: "Anyway, that was about all the information Skip had. I got it second hand from Tommy this morning before we opened. I had wandered over to the Exchange to see if they had yesterday's paper. We are out and I needed the Safeway ad. I didn't get it but got all kinds of Valley gossip instead."

Claire went on: "Last night Tommy got belted with a pool cue by a Biker. Tommy got it right across his upper back, almost his neck and head: just for winning a pool game from a poor loser. He hit Tommy hard enough to break the cue. Tommy should maybe not play pool with Bikers. Well, then Don took exception to the broken pool cue and punched the guy up a little before throwing him out, literally throwing him out the door and off the porch. Then he kicked the bike over and stomped the fenders. I guess the guy was pissed but not pissed enough to take on Don. Tommy said the guy couldn't get the bike started and pushed it down the road so he could bump start it on the downhill."

Claire continued: "Don can be an awesome guy when Tommy is involved. I never saw that side of Don before: not that I saw it, Tommy told me about it this morning: he was proud of Don. Anyway, back to this young guy from Fargo who was asking a lot of questions. He asked Skip about the booze deliveries on the Coleville, and Skip said the guy seemed to know when and how much we were hauling. Tommy relayed that part of the news to me. He also asked me if we were flying drugs. I said NO, we were not! I told Tommy that you were just flying a little booze to the Slope around the check points or road blocks or whatever you call them. When Skip showed up later in the day I asked him why he was telling Tommy about this and not me? Skip said, he didn't want me to get scared. So I asked: why were you telling Tommy about it? What business was it of his? Skip said, "Sorry, I just know Tommy looks after you when Josh is away. So I told Skip whether you are here or away I take care of myself very well, thank you. I told him, don't ever think I can't take care of myself, don't ever! I think I may have scared him a little, poor Skip. So he knew I was pissed but I think he might've also had a few too many, so I backed off and he ended up buying me dinner while Jean closed up the store. Had a nice steak, a fillet, it was yummy! Then this morning David Littlejohn, the kid, calls. He talks like he knows me and says, he's coming out to see Josh and he better not give me any lip. I told him that the only lip he'd get here would be a fat one. Pretty good comeback, don't you think? I got a million of them. Then just after you arrive from your overnighter, he shows up in that Cub with his dad, I don't get it. I have no understanding of what's going on. It has to be more than competition for the whiskey sales. I know it's good money but it's not that good. I don't know but I'm telling you if that little prick gets in my face again, he's going to have one less nut, and I don't need Angel to protect me, though she was awesome"

Angel heard her name and waged her tail: I'm glad to be home, when do we eat?

As Claire continued with the story, Josh put the events

in order, but they still made no sense.

Josh: "You're right, there's more going on than whiskey sales. It's got something to do with the mining effort up where I make the whiskey deliveries. Like I said, our next delivery will be to the real airstrip I told you about, twenty miles down river, near the strip mining, but it isn't a strip mine."

Claire just took another sip, and another, and another. Then she said, "You already told me about the new place to deliver the booze. Keep going. That David Littlejohn pisses me off. This is the son of the same guy you fed coffee to a few days ago, and I thought he seemed pretty nice. I guess he is a nice guy, and so is his son. He just gave me a 9mm Glock that he won't get back. He's probably just having a bad day."

Josh said, "Good day or bad day, I don't care. Yes, he seemed OK to me too. I'm not intimidated. He can't threaten us. He sure as hell will stay out of our delivery business now."

Josh wanted a drink and wanted to think. He also wanted Angel to stay close to Claire for awhile, real close.

Josh said, "Ok, so that was what this is all about. Angel took out the kid and you belted the father. What a truly screwed up mess this is turning into."

Josh headed to the bathroom, saying, "Fix me a glass too, will you please? Never mind, I can get my own, looks like your hand might need professional help, and don't look at me in that tone of voice. I'm just a poor lonely Bush Pilot with no malice in my heart, I need to pee."

Claire: "Just stand back a little, Superman, so you don't shatter the porcelain."

After the Black Jack hit the ice cubes, the conversation turned mild. Claire finally asked if he wanted to go next door for dinner. Josh declined the invitation: he wanted time to think. Angel on the other hand was happy to eat wherever: so where is it? Is it not dinner time?

Josh sat at the table sipping his whiskey, looking out the window, trying to put it all together: he had more questions than answers but at least he knew who the bad guys were.

After a long period of thought Josh asked, "What the heck could you find that had any value up on the Coleville with a loader and a sluice, other than gold. I don't think there has ever been a gold strike there. Any ideas?"

Claire had the same thoughts. She wondered what they were missing. If it was gold placer deposits they were seeking, they'd be farther south nearer the hills, not on the flats nearing the delta areas. She said, "What do you think's in the packages you've been taking back and forth?"

Josh decided then and there to find out what the heck he'd been delivering. He'd assumed it was paperwork, payroll, billings to check, or lists of materials they needed or something. Now that he really thought about it, the packages made no sense. The next delivery might answer the question, for sure!

Josh was up early the next day. It was warm and quiet in the valley. The chain saws across the street had been silent for a few days. It rained a little in the evening before displaying a beautiful rainbow to the south east. It was a Tuesday, generally a slow sales day, and Jean said that she and the new clerk could handle the store just fine if Claire and Josh wanted the day off.

Angel would also have an off day. She could guard the store and also grab a little sleep under the swing on the porch. Life could be real good if those bad guys would just stay away.

Claire and Josh found themselves with relaxation time on their hands and decided to fly to the Hot Springs up the Chena River Valley. They could get there early before the tour buses and the wide eyed tourists arrived.

Claire grabbed their swimming suites, a couple of towels, and was buckled up before Josh got the preflight done. In less than half an hour they were flying east toward Chena Hot Springs, looking forward to a quiet lazy day. Josh turned the radio dial to 122.9 and pushed the button on the yoke.

Josh: "Hot Springs traffic, this is silver Cessna 4 out on long final landing straight in runway 08."

After his radio work, with no other planes at the small strip, Josh lined up for a straight in landing, but he parked well away from the run up ramp. He hated when his plane got dusted with sand and gravel from other pilots doing their run ups without regard to aircraft behind them. Josh wondered if maybe he was getting just a little critical of other folks: maybe.

The hot springs opened at 8:00 and besides a pretty large pool there were five hot tubs with water quite a bit hotter than the pool. The roof over the pool was well ventilated and the sulfur dioxide smell was minimal.

They soaked in the mineral rich hot tubs for a while and got pretty relaxed. Josh suggested renting a cottage and staying for the night. Claire said she was not the cottage type but thought the idea was sweet and a little romantic. Josh smiled and almost went to sleep before Claire said she was hungry.

Then they jumped into the cooler pool and woke up a bit. They found themselves in a gentle world between total relaxation and sleepy reality, but the tour buses would arrive in an hour, and life would get back to normal soon enough. They stayed a little longer, fooling around, splashing, cavorting, dunking each other and having more fun than they'd had in a long time. Still, they knew they'd be trapped on the road back to reality soon. They left the pool and showered with fresh water, changed their clothes, and changed attitudes slowly, back to those of run of the mill General Store owners.

They decided on an early lunch at the Hot Springs Lodge. The food was expensive but well presented and delicious, according to Claire. Josh didn't give a hoot about presentation and said it'd be hard to screw up a BLT and fries. Claire noted that when it came to food Josh could screw up most anything.

The server was a part time University Student: a coed with a Masters in Physics. She had her sights set on a PhD and was studying Upper Atmospheric Chemistry in the very high latitudes, the Auroral Zone. Her name was Casey and she wanted to investigate and understand the chemistry involved with the disassociation of Refrigerant Gases, mainly Freon, in the upper atmosphere. These gases seem to be unevenly distributed, more concentrated in the lower latitudes near the equator. Casey wanted to investigate, to know exactly why and what the mechanism was.

Claire understood what Casey was talking about but Josh was only interested in why the sulfur dioxide in the pool smelled so bad. Unhappy with the long drive out to the hot springs every day, Casey mentioned she was looking for part time work closer to the University. She'd been unable to find any.

This sounded great to Claire. She told Casey if she wanted she could come by the Golden Valley Store and interview for part time work. The job would pay minimum wage plus three bucks an hour. No benefits but very flexible hours. Casey got her medical insurance thru the U of A: what other benefits were there? She said she would come by tomorrow morning at 10:00 if that was OK. It was.

After pool time and a quiet lunch, Josh and Claire were both relaxed and ready to fly home and maybe check out each other's tan lines. Besides, the first of the tour buses had arrived and a hoard of camera laden tourists speaking Asian Dialects mostly were rapidly descending on the gift shop and pool.

While Josh did his pre-flight he noticed three other planes that had flown, in when he and Claire were at lunch or in the pool: a Cessna 172, a Piper Arrow, and a Super Cub. The Cub looked too familiar: why were they following Josh now?

## Chapter Fourteen

### — *Chena Hot Springs to FIA: an Adventure* —

Josh next did his walk around. He cleaned the windshield, after checking the oil, and inspected the tire pressure. He was officially "tire sensitive" now. He thought that if he'd checked the tires before the accident, he'd have recognized the trouble instead of almost wrecking his plane: it bugged him enough that it would not happen again.

He fired the engine, checked the brakes and controls for freedom, and flipped on the alternator, the electrical master, and one radio. As he taxied to the turnaround he did a running magneto check and exercised the prop. Josh did a visual of the final approach. Seeing it was clear, he announced his takeoff to the west. He'd forgotten the runway number so he just said on 122.9: "Chena Hot Springs Traffic: Cessna 99240 Alpha starting takeoff run west. Will execute a straight out toward Fairbanks: Hot Springs traffic."

With the mixture and prop full forward and the throttle almost full, the 185 jumped ahead and was in the air in less than 400 feet. He trimmed out the plane and relaxed as the 185 flew its self right down the Chena River Valley at about 600 feet. The flight was smooth, the air warm, and both Claire and Josh still felt relaxed and looking foreword to some fun time in the afternoon under the sheets.

It happened quickly: just as Josh was gaining altitude, the elevator control on the yoke went limp, the elevator was no longer connected to the control yoke. Then the rudder control peddles went limp and useless. There was no rudder or elevator response to the controls either: This isn't possible and it, well, this isn't good!

On take-off, Josh had trimmed out the 185 well. It was just about flying itself, so it continued west. Josh added a bit of power, the nose came up some, and the plane gained a little altitude: Josh let it rise to 1000 feet above the valley floor before backing the throttle to level off. The prop was still set full "take off" and he left it alone. The aileron control seemed OK but the elevator trim was still not effective. The rudder trim seemed OK but it was the least important control input. Josh banked a little left to stay over the road as he tried to find out just how much control he did have.

Claire wasn't licensed to fly but she had stick and rudder training with Horace Black, who'd given her duel instruction before she made the decision not to pursue a pilot's certificate. She probably had enough training to fly in clear weather but in an emergency, landing a 185 without bending anything was questionable.

Josh mentioned to Claire that there might be a little problem: she wondered if they had left their bathing suits at the hot springs or maybe forgot one of the credit cards.

Josh: "No, this a little more immediate."

"Are we low on gas?"

"No, we are low on control"

That made no sense to Claire and she blew it off: she seemed to be preoccupied with taking what she hoped would be really nice pictures of Tacks General Store as they flew over Pleasant Valley at mile 23 on the Hot Springs Road.

She said, "I will give these to Cindy if they come out as well as I think. The light is just perfect. She'll like them."

Josh said, "Please put that damn camera down and do not disturb my concentration. I have almost no control over this wonderful airplane: if we hit turbulence we won't get back to the airport. I'm doing my best to see how much control there is, and it seems like very little."

Josh" "Fairbanks Tower, this Cessna 99240 Alpha."

Tower: "Cessna 99240 Alpha go ahead."

Josh: "I'm 20 miles west over the Little Chena flats above the Hot Springs Road. I have lost elevator and rudder control on a Cessna 185. I am west bound at 1000 feet at 95 knots. There are two souls aboard. I am declaring an emergency: I am inbound for landing on 1 left from the south." "Please advise clearance."

Tower: "Cessna 99240 Alpha, this is Fairbanks Tower: do you have any control over your altitude?"

Josh: "I have no elevator or vertical trim control, only a power change and flaps will allow me to change altitude. I have aileron control and rudder trim only."

Tower: "40 Alpha: can you fly past the airport, turn 180 and approach from the south?"

Josh "That is the plan: I will fly to the east away from populated areas and make a broad turn toward FAI over the flats: I will try to come in over the river and I will be very, very low over the lights."

Tower: "Eielson Center has you and is aware of your situation: frequency change to 127.2 and advise Center of your plans."

Josh: "Eielson Center, 40 Alpha is steady at 1000 feet going to 700 as soon as I clear the river going west: I will try to hold there until I make the 180 turn at Clear Creek Butte. It should be OK, if there is no turbulence: 40 Alpha"

Center: "40 Alpha, squawk 1977 and ident."

Josh: " Roger Center: squawk 1977: ident now."

Josh turned the numbers into the transponder, pushed the Ident button, and put together a plan. It might work, or not. As he reduced power, the plane would lose altitude but slow down only slightly. Unless he'd a way of trimming the nose up, a landing would be too fast and a disaster. He needed a way to trim the nose up without increasing power. His only option was to shift weight aft, to the back of the plane.

Josh told Claire to take off her harness and climb over the rear seating into the cargo area. Then he told Claire how to pull the pins out of the seat tracks: to remove the right front passenger seat and put it behind the pilot's seat. While she did this, Josh used the throttle to keep the plane in trim. His mind wandered to the possible cause of the control loss.

He just started to make the turn when Eielson Center said they had the Cessna over Clear Creek Buttes at 650 feet and 90 knots. Center advised him to commence a 140 degree three minute right turn. Josh started a very slow, less than 10 degree banked turn, to the right. He asked Claire to move up a couple of feet. She crawled forward. He increased the throttle a smidgen. A few minutes on, Eielson advised another standard right turn to a heading of 10 degrees magnetic. Josh complied, turned on his second radio, dialed it to 118.3, called Fairbanks tower, and advised he would cross the river in four minutes.

Eielson Center dumped him back to Fairbanks Tower and wished him "Good Luck."

Tower: "40 Alpha cleared to land on either runway, the airport is clear of traffic, it is not necessary to respond."

He told Claire to be prepared to move fore or aft pretty damn quick if asked but for now "just sit still where you are."

Josh pulled off a little more power and trimmed the nose a bit left. There was a right to left cross wind and he dropped the right wing a couple of degrees. They were crossing the river at 300 feet and 75 knots on short final when he told Claire to move as far back as she could. When she did, the nose came up a little, and Josh pulled on 15 degrees of flaps. This took the nose down a bit and he went to full left trim on the rudder and dropped the right wing a little more, just a very little. But it was enough to slip the 185 into the cross wind and straighten out the drift. The airspeed dropped off, as they passed the threshold at 30 feet and 60 knots. Josh cut the power back to idle and pulled 40 degrees of flaps. That was too much and he released it back to 30. They settled at 100 feet per minute, maybe a little too much, but the plane was reasonably stable. At 10 feet off the runway he told Claire to get as far back as she could and the 185 settled on the runway slightly tail first but in almost a perfect three point.

Josh, pleased, smiled. There was a little problem slowing the 185 down while keeping it on the runway: all he had was the use of the brakes and no tail wheel steering. Just the same he departed the runway left at the mid field.

Tower: "40 Alpha is off the active runway 1 left":

He then changed to ground frequency 121.9 and said, "Fairbanks Ground, Cessna 99240 Alpha is on west side, request taxi clearance to the Northwinds Aviation hanger"

Ground: "40 Alpha is cleared to taxi at will: Great job 40 Alpha, would you please stop by the tower before leaving the airport, there will be some forms to fill out in regards to your declared emergency."

Josh: "Did I declare an emergency? Must have been a slip of the tongue, can you just erase the tapes?"

Ground: "Very funny Josh, come see us!"

Josh: "Roger, will do after I inspect aft control cabling: see you in an hour."

Ground: "40 Alpha, an NTSB representative will meet you at the hanger to inspect the aircraft."

Josh: "40 Alpha."

Josh was surprised that the NTSB (National Transportation Safety Board) had a local employee at the airport. But he'd be happy to have help inspecting the 185. Claire was quite cool during the landing: she seemed to have more faith in Josh than he had in himself. Either that or she didn't entirely understand the situation. But as she thought about it, rather than being afraid, she got angry. Like Josh, she suspected sabotage of the plane, not bad maintenance. Claire was convinced that this sort of control loss was almost impossible, without some very bad outside forces.

# CHAPTER FIFTEEN

## — BAD FLIGHT, GOOD LANDING —

THEY TAXIED to the hanger, where the folks at Northwinds were waiting and already had a spot inside for the 185. Northwinds had performed the Annual and 100 hour inspections over the years and they were very worried that they might be charged with something or another involving the plane's maintenance.

Like most repair facilities, if one of their repaired aircraft had a serious problem, it would be investigated and if they were found at fault they might be sued by the aircraft owners or the FAA might restrict their licensing for a period of time, or forever: depending on the degree of negligence.

They had followed the radio traffic and treated Claire and Josh like minor celebrities who had just won a wrestling match with an alligator.

One of the younger mechanics offered to take Claire out to the Valley for her van if she needed a lift. The Director of Maintenance, Jonny Beard, was already crawling into the rear of the plane, trying to get a look at the problem before the NTSB inspector got there, but he was too late.

The NTSB inspector arrived in an official FAA car, wearing an official FAA hat, and he had an official scowl on his official face.

Josh was not about to take shit from anyone, except maybe the NTSB. When it came to aviation these guys were the biggies. He said, "Hi, I had a small problem with my flight controls and have no insight into it other than they don't work. They feel like they're disconnected in the tail section. The ailerons seem to be just fine, I think."

The inspector asked Josh to please waggle the ailerons, and Josh reached in thru the window and turned the yoke: only one aileron moved.

The inspector introduced himself as Maury FitzGerald. He said he wasn't stationed in Alaska but was here looking into a recent calibration problem of the Big Delta Vortac. The VOR is near Allen Air force Base, next to FT Greely, very near Delta Junction, 100 miles down the Richardson Highway toward Valdez. Josh asked if the VOR was not an FAA thing and Maury looked him Right Square in the eye and said, "The NTSB is interested in all aircraft related failures of navigation aids, including the failures of the FAA equipment. When investigating accidents they do work for us you know!" Wow! Let's not piss this guy off.

Jonny Beard crawled backed out of the 185 and, without even taking off his sport jacket, Maury crawled right back in where Jonny had been. He called out once for a flashlight and once for some clean rags. He spent enough time in there that the crew wondered if he was maybe taking a short nap.

When he finally crawled back out, he asked who Josh had gotten on the wrong side of. Maury told Josh and the Northwinds mechanics that it for sure wasn't wear and tear or faulty maintenance that caused this incident. Jonny felt relief knowing he hadn't been responsible.

Maury said he saw the same kind of damaged cables years ago while looking into a crash site in North Dakota. That plane had been a Cessna 182. It went down, with only the pilot, but with the same type of control cable damage. To him Josh's 185 looked like a fairly clever carbon copy of the control cable sabotage he had investigated once before.

Maury asked for the under wing inspection plates to be removed so he could see the aileron cables. One of these cables, the left hand one, was badly oxidized and had parted: only the right hand aileron cable was undamaged but had a strip of plastic electrician's tape hanging from it. Josh had landed the plane with only one working wing control surface: he was in shock, knowing Claire was correct to call it sabotage. He wondered how soon she'd be showing up to take him back to the Valley.

Maury then said he was there as a visitor, with no official

97

standing, until or if the investigation was assigned to him.

He repeated: He'd seen the type of damage before, that he found now, and it wasn't an accident then either. It was a dire warning: Josh caught that because Maury threw it.

Maury said that the FAA Controllers wanted to see Josh in the tower before he left the airport. He said, other folks would be in contact with both Jonny and Josh and it'd be best not to remove and replace anything related to the cables until the damage was documented. He said, "You may look to determine what needs to be repaired but you may not remove, or repair anything on this aircraft. Do not turn a wrench on this plane until it is properly documented."

Josh found a chair and asked if anyone had a soft drink. The mechanic said he'd take pictures of the damage in the tail: how did Josh want him to continue? Josh asked them to do no more except, yes, please do take the pictures. He might need them when he filed a Police report and also for the insurance claim. He said he wanted to talk to the FAA first and foremost.

He started walking to the tower but Jonny stopped him to drive him over in the golf cart. Then he said for Josh to just take the cart: it'd be safe, because golf carts didn't have cable steering.

While Josh talked to the FAA, Jonny Beard inspected the sabotage and came up with the fact that the control cables had been cut with a modified cable cutter, that cut all but a few center strands. It seemed then that a 4" long plastic jumbo soda straw, filled with oxidizing acid, $H_2SO_4$ (battery acid) probably, and with the ends plugged by maybe bees wax, was laid next to the partially cut cable and taped. Then the cables were pulled together and over wrapped with a single layer of plastic electricians tape. Because the cables lay next to one another the straws that carry the acid would either rupture or blow out the wax plugs when the cables pulled in opposite directions, as happened when the pilot worked the controls. The cable would then be bathed in the acid. Depending on temperature and how well the acid wet the cable it might take five minutes to half an hour for the cable to oxidize away: but corrode it would, breaking the cable apart.

Pilots fully exercise the controls prior to takeoff. Josh usually did, maybe not as fully or completely as he might have. Or the acid wrap on the right wing cables wasn't applied exactly right. Whatever the reason, the acid didn't sever the right cables, and Josh was able to land the 185 with one aileron and a prayer. The cable damage happened behind inspection plates, and Jonny guessed that an experienced person might need less than five minutes with a battery powered screwdriver and a roll of plastic tape to sabotage the cables.

When Josh returned from his talk with the FAA without the golf cart. Josh said he'd forgotten it next to the tower. Jonny sent his newest mechanic to fetch it, it was only a thousand yards or so.

Jonny Beard pretty much had the scoop right. He was fairly certain, no, he was absolutely certain, what had happened. Josh listened and was impressed. Josh always knew Jonny was a great mechanic, but his billings were equally smart.

Claire and Angel arrived with the van, as if the whole family should be together after this. She and Josh hugged and Angel jumped up, put her paws on Josh's shoulders and licked his nose. Angel knew something had gone very wrong. It might be alright now, but she remained guarded.

Josh filled Claire in on Jonny's detective work. They knew who had sabotaged the plane. With that issue resolved, the high tension dissolved. Claire and Josh weren't fearful, just ready to hurt someone, or two someones.

Claire drove the van into the hanger and unloaded the plane of anything that wasn't bolted down, their clothes bag, the survival kit and rifle, and the fire extinguisher: she even took the passenger seat. Along with the log books were extra sunglasses and Sectional Charts that the FAA insisted should be in the plane to be legal. Claire wondered when the 185 would be repaired and flying again: their business needed a plane. Jonny said it could sit in the hanger for a few days with no charge. He wished Josh luck and said he wanted to close up for the day because he had a date with a sandwich and a beer or three. Josh wanted to talk about the repairs and said he would buy Jonny dinner if he'd come out to Ivory Exchange but Jonny begged off. Actually he had a hot or somewhat hot date, and was eager to find out which.

---

## CHAPTER SIXTEEN

### — *THE FBI: WHO DID THE DEED?* —

THE STORE CLOSED at 9:00 pm. The Durable Duo went next
door for a late night dinner at the Ivory Exchange. Josh ordered
a rare New York steak, bone in, mainly because Angel liked
the meat scraps, not because he hungered so much for steak.
Claire had a Valley Bacon Burger and a dinner salad. Angel
was not quite sure what she did to get a beef bone, but she
liked it and tried to share it with Claire, who didn't quite understand how really great bones were.

The conversation centered on filling out forms. Declaring
an emergency isn't an everyday occurrence: the FAA wants to
know What, Where, When, and Why. Josh decided just to say
there'd been a control cable failure, and then wait to see what
else the FAA might need to know.

Claire wanted to get the plane repaired as soon as possible
or get another plane, without waiting for an insurance claim to
be submitted and processed. Claire said she'd borrow money
if necessary; they had to keep the business going. There was no
argument, no disagreement, just a discussion on what to do
next, how to proceed, how to handle an unresolved situation.

Claire was the business head of the partnership, and Josh
might argue a little, but he knew, when it came to the General
Store or the cargo flying and delivery business, Claire's opinions
were almost always correct.

The bar clock chimed 10:00. Too wired to sleep, Josh and
Claire ordered a second decaf and Kahlua and drank slowly.
The clicking of pool balls broke the silence. Skip arrived: he
entered the restaurant thru the massive double doors and
strolled toward the bar in a grand manner. Only music would
have made for a more noticed and regal entrance. When he got
close to the bar he pretended to trip and stumble and to catch
himself with the lanyard that rang the "drinks for the house"
bell.

That woke the place up! Skip was at that very moment, the most popular person in the Gold Stream Valley. Skip loudly and profanely proclaimed, "There are many paths but only one truth." Josh wondered, what the hell did that mean and what is he doing here at this time of night?

Tommy and Skip then held a loud disagreement about the "Drinks on the House Bill". Skip agreed with the number but insisted that Tommy add 20% as a gratuity. Tommy said it was not fair to tip the "Beer Keeper", who was Tommy, because he was also drinking, and probably had more than one.

Tommy suggested they play a game of 8 ball to decide the disagreement. Skip consented to the contest but argued as to who would supply the quarter for the pool table. Skip finally paid and racked up the balls: not too surprisingly Tommy ran the table. The outcome was that no tip was included in the bill: that was settled, but then Skip wanted his quarter back. This could only happen in the Gold Stream Valley.

Later, near midnight, Skip wandered over to the Durable Duo, now on their fourth after dinner cocktail and asked how badly the plane was damaged.

Josh asked, "How the hell did you find out about that?"

Skip: "I've my sources. Was it really vandalism?"

Claire: "Vandalism hell, it was attempted murder and when I catch the guilty it will be murder for real."

Skip explained that he saw Jonny Beard, depressed and producing alligator tears at Skip's bar in the city. Jonny was deflated by the unsuccessful outcome of a date he had with Ms. Wonderful, who thought Jonny was Mr. awful. After consoling words and a complimentary beer, Jonny spilled the whole story on the 185. Claire had asked Jonny not to spread it around but it was good that Skip already knew the details. She'd decided to seek his council on how to proceed.

Skip had called the store. No answer meant Josh and Claire were probably at the Exchange for dinner and solace. Skip was aware that Josh wanted a Cessna 206 and said he knew of a well-off junior wannabe bush pilot who thought he really needed a 185, but had a newer 206, but thought the nose wheel was not complimentary to his desired persona. Skip recommended that Josh take a look at a possible deal, a swap with a few bucks to boot.

Skip said the 206 had a 3 axis auto pilot, King radios, duel Omni, a DME, it was full IFR and had almost every other accessory a guy could think of including long range tanks. Josh said he'd talk to the guy but thought the 206 would be too expensive; also the 185 was not presently airworthy. Just the same Claire said, "Go for it, at least see if it'd be a good plane for us." Josh and Skip agreed to meet on the East Ramp at FAI at 11:00 am tomorrow and, if they could find the 206, kick the tires.

With that Skip left and Josh realized that Skip had come all the way out to the Valley just to tell him about the 206. He also knew that Claire had wanted him to have a better cargo plane and she wanted him to stop landing on places that a good pilot should not be going. He knew it was just a matter of time before he bent his plane badly getting in or out of places he should not be in the first place. Josh wondered if maybe Skip and Claire were in a little conspiracy involving the proposed airplane swap: he thought maybe it might be a good idea.

Claire said that the store was making pretty good money on the Fire Box Contract, feeding the Firefighters at Rosie Creek. The fire was a hard fought campaign and the store sold many more meals than she'd expected. The billings were in excess of $65,000.00 with more still coming. Their margin was around 40%: that isn't hay!

Josh had made a bunch of bucks with the recent whiskey deliveries also, and Claire said she'd be able to scratch out a few extra bucks, if the 206 looked good and the price was right. Claire also dropped the bomb shell that the 185 had just finally been paid off this month: almost poetic.

Josh had a headache when he woke Thursday morning,

and his hair hurt. He could hear Claire's voice down in the store dealing with a laundromat problem, and Jean tending to customers at the checkout counter, and he had slept in: it was 9:00. By his normal schedule it was afternoon. Josh wondered how much he really had to drink. He looked out the window over the back porch and it looked lonely out there without his trusty 185 looking back at him. Josh had a cup of coffee and no breakfast. He scraped the moss off his teeth with a wire brush, or at least it felt like it, and sauntered down the inside stairs to the store. How the hell had he slept in that long?

About the time he hit the store, Jean answered the phone and handed it to him.

Jean: "Someone is talking 90 miles an hour and thinking at 35: It must be for you, flyboy."

Jean sometimes considered herself to be the second boss at the store and treated Josh like the hired help. She had no tolerance for folks that drank too much: and last night he had.

The call was from Jonny Beard at Northwinds: He was as excited as Josh had ever known him to be. He said, two guys from - and he whispered, the FBI - would probably be showing up at the store soon: he wanted to give Josh a heads up and then pumped him for information which Josh was sure would get back to Skip at just slightly less than the speed of light. What was he going to do, hide? Jonny thought Josh and Claire might be in some pretty big trouble but Josh knew what the problem was. Aircraft sabotage, Commercial or Private, is a federal crime: it is not trivial!

Josh guessed that the NTSB inspector, Maury FitzGerald, had contacted the local FBI office with information about yesterday's control cable incident on the Cessna 185.

The Fairbanks FBI office had opened a few years back, shortly after the pipe line permits were finalized and issued to subcontractors. Before that it had been a part time place only manned when there was a local problem. It seemed that folks from the Anchorage office who needed some discipline were sent to Fairbanks when there was a local federal issue, usually in the winter months. Josh thought he once heard, there were three agents in town. He did not know what they normally did, but guessed it might've just gotten interesting.

Josh called the contact number that Skip had given him and asked Matt Smith, the owner of the 206, if he'd meet them at FAI at 11:00. Matt gave him the location, the tail number, and described the plane.

A half hour later a pair of extremely well dressed, polite gentlemen in perfectly tailored black suits, complete with wrap-around sun glasses, walked into the Golden Valley General Store and asked for the Owner/Operator, if he was available. They wished to speak to Mr. Joshua Jordan Browning, or his legal representative. Josh had seen several movies about the FBI and thought maybe the movies had nailed the appearance of the agents perfectly: they were beautiful! One looked like Efrem Zimbalist Jr and the other spoke like a kingly version of Jack Webb. Angel sniffed them both: she was guarding. Josh thought: this is going to be an experience!

The FBI Special Agents introduced themselves, and then asked a few questions about plane and control cables. Mike Thompson said he was the Special Agent in Charge and asked the questions. The other agent, Noel Simpson, was quiet and spent some time scratching Angel's ears. Angel only tolerated the ear scratch: she was unimpressed. Both were smooth and trying, maybe too hard, to be pleasant and not confrontational.

When Josh described the method of sabotage, the agents nodded to each other, and Josh realized something more was going on. It seemed like a play with bad acting. Maybe this was just a secondary investigation of a bigger scene.

Josh said he had to meet a friend at the airport at 11:00 and did the agents want to see the cable issue in person: the plane was parked inside the Northwinds Aviation facility. Josh knew they'd already seen the plane: Jonny Beard had called and said so. So it wasn't surprising that they begged off, saying they'd get back to him later if they needed additional info. Josh wondered what that was all about but figured it'd work out somehow.

As they started to leave, Claire walked over to ask what she and Josh might do to help the FBI investigation, and just who was supervising the Fairbanks office. She insisted on the contact information: she was not going to be ignored.

Mike said, "We are special investigators from District Headquarters; the local office is not involved in this investigation. The local office may not even know we are here: this is a 'need to know' investigation."

Claire said sharply, "Sabotage of airworthy aircraft is against several federal laws. I want this investigated. I expect an arrest and prosecution of the people who committed this crime. You work for me, damn it. Get to work on this, now."

Mike Thompson turned to Josh.

Josh: "Don't look at me for help. If I have to solve this problem it might not be pretty. I don't have a shiny gold shield to hide behind. We've a good idea who did the deed and you never even asked. What the hell's going on? Are you really with the FBI?"

Noel and Mike conferred some and finally said: "We want to see the damage to the plane ourselves and then make the determination whether it is actually sabotage or just normal wear and tear."

Josh: "You've already seen the plane so stop being stupid."

Jean had been in the back store room listening and felt she had to add to the conversation. She walked around the counter and, though completely uninvited, also asked if the agents were really FBI, and if they were which country was their bureau affiliated with? And that was just the start.

Jean said, "I'm very unhappy with your attitude and will report your actions to the district office if the investigation doesn't proceed, post haste. Do you know what Professionalism means? These people were almost killed yesterday and you seem afraid of getting your pretty black suits dirty. Do your damn job!"

Jean really liked Claire and Josh. They were much more than just her employers. She felt protective of them because they'd defended her when she needed support. Jean was not to be underestimated, she was loyal and a lot smarter than the average 38 year old General Store Clerk. Mike Thompson tried to get a word in but was unable. After being chewed out by Claire and now by Jean, the poor guy was about exhausted.

Mike: "OK, OK, we'll start the paperwork for an investigation. We'll be at the Northwinds Hanger at 7:00 tomorrow morning."

Josh: "Make it at 8:00, that's when they open."

Mike: "Fine. Dammit, 8:00 it will be."

# Chapter Seventeen

## — New Planes: Old Problems —

WITH THE PROMISE of an investigation Claire had done all she could to speed repair of the 185. Now all she had to do was wait: she hated to wait. Josh was meeting up with Skip and the 206 owner. Claire decided to stay at the store, though Friday store traffic would be slow: if they rang $1,400.00 on a Friday it'd be a really great sales day. Still, she could interview Casey if and when she stopped by, then drive her jeep to the airport for a look at the 206, then come back and relieve Jean before the beer rush at 5:00: Jean had a life to, don't you know!

Casey did arrive on time and, after being introduced to Jean, got down to particulars. Claire asked questions about other job experiences and was pleased with the answers.

Claire: "Why do you want the job?"

Casey: "I need the money, I think you said three dollars on top of minimum wage: is that correct?"

Claire: "Yes, to start. When you show you can handle the store by yourself, the pay will be twice minimum wage. The only benefit I can offer is free use of the laundromat and shower facility, for you only, not your friends. Jean is our store manager. You'll work for me but be supervised by her. You'll be on probation for forty hours, to see if you fit in. What say?"

Casey: "You said, hours are flexible. What could they be?"

Claire: "That's between you and Jean. She's easy to please if you say what you will do and then do as you say. If that sounds OK, when would you like to start?"

Casey: "Right now if you wish, I have a phone call to make: can I use the store phone?"

Claire "Yes, of course." "Jean, you've help for the rest of the day, OK? The Firefighters will need 12 more food boxes. Show Casey how to stuff them but leave out the meat and perishables. Just stack them in back and I can finish the packing if we get the order later tonight. Also, do an inventory of the fire box food stuffs. Is that enough to keep you busy for the rest of the day? I have to meet Josh."

Jean: "Of course: have a great day. Don't I have to walk the dog too?"

Claire: "Is that sarcasm?"

Angel heard that Dog word and waged her tail but other than that lay quietly under the swing.

Claire backed her jeep out of the car port and was set to leave, when Carter Thomas drove in and parked between the store. Claire shut the jeep off and walked to Carter.

Carter: "I heard from Skip that you had some problem with the 185: what happened?"

Claire: "Someone sabotaged the plane while we were soaking our buns at the Hot Springs yesterday morning. It looks like Jim Littlejohn, or his crew did it. Josh saw their Super Cub parked there as we were leaving. We almost didn't get back. You can get the story from Josh later if you want."

Carter: "Is the plane going to be repaired soon, I hoped to set up a delivery for next Wednesday: that gives you five days to get the 185 up and flying."

Claire: "This is Friday. No, I don't think it can be repaired by then. The NTSB told us to do nothing until the incident is fully documented."

Carter: "Can you rent a plane? We can probably stand for the price of a rental."

Claire: "Josh and Skip are on the East Ramp as we speak, kicking the tires and looking at a 206."

Carter: "If you guys want to buy it, my company will pre-pay for deliveries. We might go as high $20,000.00 on a hand-shake, no interest if repaid within the year."

Claire said thank you and that she'd relay the offer to Josh within the hour. ""Is the number we have for Pete the best way to get to you?" she asked.

Carter said no, and gave her another number to call.

Carter: "Pete shouldn't know that I offered financial help

to you guys: in fact he should never know." Well, that was odd.

Claire promised to get back to him by noon tomorrow. She asked if he wanted another delivery of a full pallet of R&R. Carter said yes, and one other small but important lock box. They shook hands, and Claire left for the airport, as Carter went to the Ivory Exchange for lunch.

Skip and Josh found Matt and his 206 on the East Ramp: it looked ready to go. The plane was quite nice, as described. After looking at the log books, Josh was eager to make a deal. The owner it turned out was not the real owner. Matt's father had a personal loan on the plane with the Bank of the North, but Matt Smith was the legal owner, according to the Title and Registration.

It was obvious right off, a Cessna 206 didn't fit Matt's wannabe persona. He needed a real bush plane to be a real bush pilot. Still, Matt's dad had made the down payment and handed his kid the keys and told him to go seek his fortune. Matt promised he'd try to fly within his skill level and his dad would someday be proud.

With that promise and the plane, and a real Commercial Pilot's license, Matt had found a job as an Assistant Guide with one of the more popular Master Guides in the Interior: Bud Hastings. The Guide told Matt he had the wrong plane, that he should get a tail dragger. He suggested a Maule 180 but Matt wanted a Cessna 185, because real Bush Pilots preferred it, or so he thought. Matt also thought an Assistant Guide position would be the best job in the world. He had no idea.

Josh recalled old movie scenes of African Safaris, where the poor black "Porters" carried all sorts of crap thru the jungle and across the crock-infested rivers. They lugged tents, set up camp, dug latrines, and attended to every wish of the Great White Hunter who sipped iced gin and tonics with his fat Banker clients. Those porters, and/or transporters who carried all the crap and did all the work for a dollar a day: they were the Assistant Guides. If Matt only knew!

Josh said the 185 could be available in two weeks, with the repairs paid in full and a fresh Annual inspection. Matt was thrilled. He'd looked at the plane before and had a real desire to own it. There were other 185s for sale, two in Anchorage in fact, but Matt liked the paint scheme and the 99240A tail number. Josh thought: this guy is unbelievable, he won't last two weeks, maybe they'll make him the camp cook.

Matt thought the 185 was worth $29,000 after repairs and a fresh annual. Just as Josh was about to answer, Skip said that was about right, but the 206 wasn't worth the $37,000 Matt was asking, so what kind of deal did he offer?

Matt wasn't a horse trader, and so far out of his element he could hardly reply. He thought for a long time and finally said, "$10,000 is a fair dollar difference between the planes. I've already checked it out with my dad."

Skip: "Sounds a bit high to us. We could live with $7,500 but we need a $1,000 for a fresh Annual inspection: planes always trade with fresh annuals. The offer is $6,500 and we trade titles.

Matt: "I will go for $8,500 but no damn annual inspection. There are other 185s out there. I feel like I'm about to get raped, and I'm not even getting a kiss. What you see is what you get, that's it: take it or leave it!"

Matt now felt he was in command and a pretty good negotiator. He might have been had he started from the right dollar amount, but he wasn't getting screwed and in fact the petting was fairly light.

Skip and Josh huddled: Josh couldn't believe the proposed deal, he was wetting his pants. Skip said he might try for another $500, but Josh said no.

Josh: "He just proposed an amazing trade; let's just take the deal before he changes his mind."

Skip: "The 206 has a few more hours on the engine and prop than the 185: we're taking a chance but we can do the trade with $8,000 to boot: remember Josh is standing all the repairs to get the 185 airworthy with a fresh annual. $8,000 is a fair trade up deal: you know that is true."

Matt: "$8,250 will do, but you guys owe me, and I won't forget."

Josh: "Deal at $8,250." They shook hands.

Skip: "What will Claire say? Does it matter?"

Josh: "It matters, but we should take the deal now. It's better to beg forgiveness than ask permission, right? How do you think I got her to marry me?"

Skip: "I don't know, but you sure as hell won big when you got her to say, I do."

Matt and Josh shook hands on the deal, as Claire arrived in her pretty silver Jeep CJ, with the top down. With her hair in disarray from the wind, she looked like she was from that Goldstream Valley.

Claire's name before she married was Jameson, Claire Jameson: "CJ". Josh thought, that's why she bought a "Jeep CJ". In the beginning, Josh had called her CJ: she did not like that. To retaliate she called him JJ: for Joshua Jordan. Josh did not like that either, so they called a lovers truce and made it a point of not using initials. Once, while living in Yakutat, when Claire was letting a school administrator have a piece of her mind, Josh intervened to calm down the explosive situation. Claire had told "JJ" to "butt the hell out of my business". After that their initials became a signal between them that something provocative was happening or about to happen.

Claire was happy with the proposed transaction. A Cessna 206 is as powerful as a 185 but quieter and far more comfortable. An empty or lightly loaded 206 is a great performer and a loaded one is an Alaskan pack mule, with a great cargo door for loading and unloading. The lack of a passenger door was trivial to Claire. Josh might have a passenger one in ten trips. And she thought the 206 looked nice, really nice and very slick.

Skip said he knew the manager of Bank of the North and one way or another he'd issue a note for $8,250.00, or Skip would loan them the cash himself. Matt didn't give a damn where they got the money. The deal was done. Claire said that the store account could cover a check for $8,250, if she put off paying for the 5,000 gallon fuel delivery and other invoices: Josh asked her to please write the check. "Now, if you please."

With the fruits of Claire's writing abilities on display, Matt and Josh traded keys and signed off the titles on the spot. Both planes had insurance policies through the Randolph State Farm Office in Fairbanks. Matt would keep his tie down spot on the East Ramp, and Josh could fly the 206 to the valley, tonight if he wanted. When the NTSB gave the OK, Jonny would make repairs to the 185: either Josh or State Farm would stand the repair bill. Jonny wanted State Farm to stand the repairs as he could hammer them a little harder than he would Josh.

Josh: "Hey Matt, did you know you were getting brand new tires, wheels, and brakes? We have the seats and duel controls at the store. Jonny will put them back in on my buck."

Matt: "Thanks, I like it as it is, but I'll pick them up with the seats after the repairs are complete." Matt kept smiling. He thought he was getting about the best cargo-carrying true bush plane there has ever been. He was pretty much correct.

Skip had gotten a lift to the East Ramp and planned to catch a ride to Goldstream with Josh after they saw the 206: neither of the men had a clue they'd make the deal today. Skip planned to meet his present Main Squeeze, Martha, at the Ivory Exchange for dinner. She'd have Skip's car. It worked out that Skip drove the store's van back to the Valley, Claire followed in the Jeep. And, after a really complete pre-flight, and pumping and paying for 63 gallons of fuel, Josh took off in one of the finest single engine propeller driven aircraft Cessna has ever produced. He loved it. Life was great!

When Skip drove into the parking lot, it felt like old times for him. He knew where to park the van so it was available for business, without taking a customer parking spot. He'd built the Store long ago and operated it before building and running the restaurant with his first wife. Skip still felt a few heart strings pulling, at some of his fondest memories. He felt close to Josh and Claire, as they now ran the business so well, that he'd started. They still provided a community phone, and the free coffee was usually hot and fresh. If not occupied, there were a few friendly chairs to sit in while drinking the coffee and maybe collecting a little of the newest Valley gossip. A bulletin board was there for the neighborhood folks, to post on. Lost dogs and found mittens were big.

Skip knew everyone in Goldstream; he was gregarious, popular, and told some of the best stories. Skip was big, handsome, friendly, full of bluster and profanity, and usually surrounded by people attracted to his larger than life persona. But sometimes, like today, he felt very much alone. He locked the van, dropped the keys off in the store, and walked over to the Exchange for a beer, and maybe a pool game with Tommy.

When Josh landed, he taxied to his regular parking place, tied the 206 down, and went straight to the Ivory Exchange to see Skip. Josh asked if he and Claire could treat Skip and Martha to dinner and drinks a little later, say maybe 8:00. Skip's face lit up like a Christmas tree. He said yes, he'd see them at 8:00.

Back at the store, Claire asked Josh about the plane, if it flew as it should. She wondered if Josh had buyer's remorse? Josh said the 206 was very quiet compared to the 185. He was quite happy, and he'd invited Skip and Martha to dinner at the Exchange. Josh also mentioned that Skip had something on his mind and that he seemed kind of sad. Claire said, "Today is the one year anniversary of Skip's third divorce. I doubt Martha will have a good time today."

# CHAPTER EIGHTEEN

### — *PREPPING FOR THE FIRST TRIP IN THE 206* —

JOSH NOTICED a different face behind the counter: it was Casey ringing the register and making small talk. Jean was in the back doing who knows what.

Claire: "While you and Skip kicked tires and spent our hard earned money on frivolous flying toys, the three of us were busy taking orders and making sales: we are here on the front lines of the battle in the continuing war of retail sales."

Josh: "You are such martyrs!"

Claire said, they had a delivery request for another pallet of R&R for next Wednesday. She'd already placed the order with P&J. "It'll be delivered Tuesday with our regular order for the store." She knew Josh wanted an excuse to fly the 206 and felt, or at least hoped, that good things were beginning again.

Claire: "By the way, the next time I see the Littlejohn Super Cub anywhere near us, I intend to shoot out the tanks and burn it where it sits. Speaking of burning, the State is now up to date with our billings for the fire box food. The check I wrote for the 206 is quite kosher: that means good, you know?"

There was lots to do now, because Department of Natural Resources (DNR) had called and wanted fourteen food boxes for the fire fighters, post haste! Jean had them pretty much complete. Josh had no sooner arrived but had to drive back into town to the University Avenue DNR facility and deliver, you guessed it: 14 fire fighter food boxes.

Each box fed six fire fighters for three days: that was a bunch of food. The Foresters unloaded the van as usual and signed the delivery invoices. On his way back Josh counted up the $42.50 profit he made on each food box: that was unless he got some of the groceries, like the canned ham, on sale. "I love it when a plan comes together!"

Claire was eager to celebrate the deal and show Skip how much they appreciated his trading skills: they met Skip and

Martha, as planned, at the Ivory Exchange. Claire figured Skip's trading skills saved them maybe $4,000, and a lot of hassle. Josh thought the figure was higher but agreed a $100 dinner was a good and proper amount because Skip might need a ride in a really fine airplane sometime and Josh was fully prepared to offer Skip a proper 25% discount on expenses.

After a great dinner of New York Strip Steak and King Crab legs, Tommy and Don came over to the table and brought Champagne: to christen the new plane. Don said they should drink the contents instead of break the bottle on the spinner of the plane and Josh agreed: the spinner was aluminum. Martha agreed with the drinking part and said they needed a couple more bottles and that Skip would pop for them. Skip seemed to get some of his Mo Jo back, as Martha acted like one of the group rather than just a date for the evening. Claire thought maybe Skip needed someone special and maybe, just maybe, he'd found someone. Claire leaned way over the table and gave Skip a big kiss on his cheek and said, "Happy Fucking Anniversary: she has no idea what she is missing."

Skip just sat there, took Martha's hand with one of his and wiped a tear from his eye with the other.

On Friday, Casey agreed to work the early shift with Claire. With store hours of 9:00 am to 9:00 pm it was a long day for anyone, so Casey worked till 5:00, an 8 hour day. Jean came in at 1:00 and worked until 9:00: an 8 hour day. Claire was there most of the time, to do inventory and ordering. That left Josh to do laundromat maintenance and other odd jobs that had to be done or the world might come to an end, or something. Josh was available to do pickups in town or bush air deliveries, as need be. He also handled extra pickups and food boxes for the fire fighters. This business was short lived but had a better margin than other profit centers in the store.

Sunday the store closed at 6:00 pm. Jean and Claire both could "have a life" Sunday evening. At least once a week, life was good, or better!

Of course schedules never worked out 100%. The part time clerk who had been with them all of 6 weeks and was about to be fired, quit. This saved Claire the agony of telling someone that their work ethic stinks, so it was for the best.

Casey added the hand that the store really needed. She could add, subtract, and make change, something the last clerk was short skilled on. Claire wondered how some people ever made it out of High School. Casey's schooling hours at UAF were three days a week in the afternoon. On those days she worked till noon. God only knows when she did her home work. Jean suggested that Claire end Casey's probation period at 24 hours and give her the pay raise immediately. Claire said she'd consider the request. Jean insisted!

Saturday morning Josh had to work the cash register while Claire did the final cigarette and cigar inventory for the Monday order. Smokes were going up to $0.70 a pack; it seemed like a lot for a smoke. Josh had never smoked but Claire had and said quitting was one of the most difficult things she'd ever done. Still with a profit of 18 cents a pack who was to argue. Tobacco was probably safer than the crap most of the Smith Road folks lit up.

Both Josh and Claire were more or less non-political and if they had taken a test to discover their politics it might have scored Libertarian. They kind of thought as long as adults hurt no one, except maybe themselves, whatever is OK, is OK with them. That's a long way of saying, "Mind your own business, and I will mind mine."

Josh was replacing a belt in the #1 dryer in the laundromat when Jonny Beard came by to ask if Josh had been in the hanger, working on the 185.

Josh said, "Of course not, I'm only qualified for dryers and washers: why?"

Jonny: "Someone worked on your plane last night, someone who can pick a lock and has the skills and tools to rip out all the damaged cables and disappear them. The NTSB guy,

Maury, had arranged to meet me at the hanger this morning, he wanted to document the damage to the control system. He had a 35mm camera with a close up lens and a tripod. There was nothing to photograph. The plane had been stripped of all, I mean all, the broken cables, and he kind of accused me of doing it. I told him as I told you; I wasn't touching it until I got the word from you, to start the repairs."

Josh: "So you are telling me that the damaged cables are gone, that they were stripped out of the plane? Was it a hacked up job?"

Jonny: "No, it was professional, the tail end of the 185 is pristine: nothing else was missing except the cables and connectors and it was swept or vacuumed cleaned. Whoever did it saved you some money, I don't have to rip out the broken parts myself now."

Josh: "It was not me. Did you know I sold the 185 and bought the 206 from Matt Smith?"

Jonny: "No I didn't, no kidding, that's a hell of a plane. Matt's dad paid me for some radio replacements and a couple of new strobes. That plane is in pretty good shape: how many hours on it, I forget?"

Josh: "640 on a Factory New engine and prop, installed at Western Skyway's a couple of years ago, and about 2,100 on the airframe. The last Annual looked good. I wanted you to look at it for me but we made the deal so quick there never was a chance."

Jonny: "It's a fine flying machine. So you know nothing about the 185? That guy Maury said he already saw the damage and knew it was for real. He was pretty pissed that you would start the work before he got the pictures. I think you'll hear from him soon."

Josh: "Other than paying you to do the control cable work, the restoration; I no longer have an interest in the plane."

Jonny: "What the hell is going on?"

Josh: "Don't know. Want a beer? I just have to button this

dryer up, should take only a minute or five. Ever thought about a career in appliance repair? The pay is poor, the hours are irregular, and I can guarantee that you'll never meet a satisfied customer."

Jonny: "I'll meet you on the bar stool closest to the pool room: meanwhile, I have to wring out a kidney."

Jonny left the laundromat and walked across the parking lot to the Ivory Exchange. Maybe he'd have a bacon cheese burger while he waited.

A small business in Fairbanks specialized in cleanup and repair of homes with fire or flood damage. Their motto was "Like it never ever happened." Josh had wondered, if damaging the control cables and inviting the FBI to the party was not well thought out, maybe some hot head had done it. But taking the damaged cables was the final proof of sabotage, and a clear way to minimize the investigation.

# Chapter Nineteen

## — *The First Trip to Stampede* —

THE STORE TRAFFIC had slowed to zero by the time Josh locked Soapies and carried his tool box back into the store. Jean had just finished inventory on the fire boxes and was ringing out the cash register, when Josh walked in followed by Angel. Angel had inspected the 206 and even though she claimed one of the tires she was not sure it was the plane for her: until a little later next morning when she saw the cargo door open, maybe then. But that's tomorrow.

Josh told Claire about the missing control cables.

Claire: "It must be the FBI guys" I knew there was something fishy about them. The guy that looked like Jack Webb: I bet he knows exactly what's going on! What do you think?"

Josh: "Not a clue, Mrs. Browning, not a clue. It might've been that Mustard character with a candle stick in the library, maybe not. For some stupid reason I'm in a very good mood all of a sudden. If you can close up by yourself, I've a pool game with Jonny next door and I want to talk to him more"

Claire: "Sure, I can handle the heavy job of toting the cash upstairs. See you in 15, but I don't want to eat there tonight. We have some really nice TV chicken dinners that got thawed and refrozen and need eating. They also are a little past their sale date, so prepare yourself for a true culinary delight."

Sitting in the bar and waiting for Josh, Jonny was in a strange mood. He thought he had let Josh down: he had no idea what had happened to the 185, and when he realized his hanger was not secure he felt as though he'd been personally violated: he was getting angry and was ready to strike out but had no one to vent his anger at.

Besides that, he was sure the FAA was going to blame him for the missing cables and he had no explanation of what might have happened. As far as he knew he and his two employees had the only keys to his hanger: Jonny totally trusted the both of them: and why the hell'd anyone steal damaged control cables out of an airplane anyway?

Josh said the answer was simple: whoever set the cables to fail wanted no evidence of the sabotage. Maury told them the same type of sabotage had happened before, years ago and many miles away in North Dakota, and whoever did the deed then probably did not want the sabotage incidents linked. The motive wasn't obvious to Jonny but Josh knew exactly who did it or paid to have it done.

Jonny Beard was less certain and really worried that the FAA believed he pulled the cables to protect himself from an investigation of his 100 hour and Annual Inspection methods. He felt the FAA was out to persecute aircraft mechanics and get most every mechanic fined or in some way disciplined for any wreck that ever happened to any plane that one had ever worked on or inspected.

He was at least partially right. The FAA did want to fix blame for every incident and accident that happened, but beyond trying to find the truth they were really only concerned with aircraft safety.

Josh and Jonny talked about the incident every which way and always came back to the FBI guys not really being FBI, and if they were not, who the heck were they? He thought they looked too much like the stereotype to be real. Maybe a whole lot more going on than was obvious. One thing Josh did know was that the next person who intentionally damage his airplane would need weeks of recuperation and physical therapy: if he survived.

Saturday was breezy and the weatherman predicted rain later in the day. Josh told Claire that he was taking the plane up to do slow flight and stall practice and touch and goes at Metro to get used to the nose wheel landings, which was a little lie, but he did practice some of the basic maneuvers on his way to see Earl Pilgrim at the Stampede Mine.

He took a half dozen oranges, two heads of lettuce, some

apples, and about any other produce he could find that might not be missed: he always brought something when visiting Earl. Josh did not fly straight to Stampede, instead he stopped at the Gold King Airstrip and watered a tree and listened for other air traffic. He listened for over an hour and heard nothing as he read the 206s Pilots Operating Handbook from cover to cover. He also enjoyed a warm Coke and a Snickers bar.

It bothered him that Carter knew so much about where he went and when. If Carter knew, maybe other folks did too. It really bothered Josh! Finally he fired up the 206 and headed to Stampede. Earl would like the fresh produce.

After landing and tie down, Josh walked the fifteen minutes to the cabin. Earl was doing his laundry, which wasn't an easy job. Even the best of Earl's equipment was old, and he had to start a hand cranked generator to power his tub style washing machine. The generator powered the washer or the well pump, but not both at the same time. He also had a wood-fired steam generator to heat water: Josh thought he might spend less time by just beating his dirty clothes on a rock. Doing the laundry was an all day affair at the Stampede mine.

With Josh there, Earl put his laundry efforts on hold. Josh asked about Jim Littlejohn. Earl said he spoke to him a while back and gave him a tour of the concentrator sheds. Earl said Littlejohn was no miner, not at all, but seemed a good Bull Shit Artist, maybe even a good Con man. Littlejohn claimed he'd get back to Earl with a lease offer but didn't. Earl wasn't surprised. He had no idea what this jerk was about, but for sure it had nothing to with the Stampede Antimony Mine.

Earl had found a new hot spring down by the west end of the airstrip, very close to the river, convenient for his weekly bath, to make his tired old bones rejuvenate some. Earl asked if Josh thought anyone could make money with a Fly in Hot Springs Resort. Josh said he wasn't sure but nobody got rich at Manley or Circle Hot Springs, and those places are both fly in and on the highway system.

Josh then told Earl about the strip mining operation that was no strip mining operation, up on the Coleville River. Earl had been around a long time and knew more about Interior Alaskan mining than anyone. Josh asked plain and simple: "What can be found of value on the Colville with a sluice?"

Earl thought, then said, "When you're back in civilization, go to the Fairbanks library, and look up Kimberlitic Pipes. You'll find that Kimberlite is an igneous rocky material that sometimes contains diamonds. Diamonds were found in Kimberlite in Canada a few years back. Hell, there could be Pipes here. In Canada, geologists back tracked a few surface diamonds to what they thought were Pipes: they were lucky as hell, because their search method was badly flawed. Initially they looked for magnetic anomalies, by flying magnetometers around in small planes like yours. On finding one, they flew in a pretty big sluice, processed several million yards of material, and came up with a few diamonds. Then they worked their way up an ancient river bed, looking for the source of the stones. It took a bunch of money and years, but, according to some folks, the approximate location of a Kimberlitic Pipe was found: rumor has it, DeBeers bought them out and closed the exploration down. It might be true, or not."

Earl continued, "The pipes are old, a hundred times older than the mountains. Diamonds are heavy, 1/3 heavier than quartz, and can be found with a sluice but you must be looking for them. A gold miner who saw raw diamonds in his sluice would think they were just quartz and toss them out. Maybe you're seeing prospecting, a search for an ancient Kimberlitic Pipe. You should be able to tell if an active search is going on. They must have tried other areas. If this spot you're talking about is on the Coleville, go a little down river and see if folks scraped the gravel there. A fly over should reveal scars in the land. Land heals very slowly in the Arctic. One other thing: you can find diamonds in the good old USA in maybe 25 spots. Finding a few diamonds isn't unusual but finding a place in the

USA with lots of diamonds, quality raw stones, has yet to be done."

They talked more and Earl gave Josh a bottle of Salmon Berry wine to take back to Claire. He promised to visit them when he got to town: he never does. He thinks he's a bother or something, but he always gets an invite anyway.

Walking back to the airstrip, Josh saw a Grizzly bear and her cub eating their way thru a Black Berry bramble. The cub got stuck pretty badly and let out a cry that sounded like a goat bleating. The mother swatted the cub. It did three summersaults before stopping. Then the cub crawled back quietly and nuzzled its mother, and got back to the job of eating. Life in the great outdoors is good for Grizzly bears in the summer. If the cub makes it till fall without meeting a male Grizzly, it should have a chance of surviving through the next winter.

Flying back to Goldstream Valley, Josh first flew to the airport at Nenana for a few touch and go and three short field landings and take offs. Nenana has a gravel strip, long and wide. Josh found the 206 flew much like the 185 but seemed more forgiving close to the ground. He got comfortable with the plane and felt he could land it where ever he wanted. From the Nenana strip, he followed the Alaska Rail Road through the hills back toward Fairbanks to Ann's Green House, where the Rail Road crosses the Murphy Dome Road. It was a training exercise that Horace Black, flight instructor, had given him long ago.

You fly at 60 miles per hour 60 feet above the track and make turns just like the train does, which is harder than you might think. At 60 knots the nearly empty plane seemed very stable in the tight turns. Josh was happy, but what he really wanted to see was how well the 206 handled with a pallet of whiskey in back. That he'd find out in a few days from now. He looked forward to the trip: wonder if Angel would want to go with.

# CHAPTER TWENTY

## — *WHISKEY RUN NORTH IN THE 206* —

TUESDAY EVENING Pete arrived with the lock box that Carter had asked Josh to deliver with the pallet of R&R. There was also a rather large cardboard box of laundry detergent and a dozen leather work gloves, the kind a Cat Skinner might wear when working on a dozer. The plane was already loaded and the cases tied down well. Turbulence can cause cargo to move around in a plane and that's asking for trouble. The 206 can carry a bunch of weight, almost 1,400 pounds, but the weight must be distributed properly or the plane won't fly properly at slow speeds. After fuel, pilot, and necessary survival gear, it is still a mini moving van. It's almost a routine thing to over load a 206 on takeoff and then burn off a few hundred pounds of fuel getting to a destination and still land the plane at near gross weight. A 206 is a work horse, one hell of a cargo hauler!

Josh decided to bring Angel along but only if she really wanted go. As he preflighted the plane she jumped around to show she was ready. I hope you do a better job landing than you did last time!

He had already strapped her harness in the passenger seat and she seemed willing to endure the "lockup" to fly with him. The last thing Josh did before takeoff was get the lock box out of the gun safe in the bedroom closet. He weighed the case on his ivory scale and pressed a very smallest grain of black pepper between the lock body and the tumbler: he recorded the weight of the box to the last tenth of a gram. Josh wondered what the heck was in it. He probably could have taken the lock box to Skip to get it opened and might at a later date. As for now it was really not his business: and he almost thought that it might be better not to know, almost, but not quite.

Josh said his "so longs" to the store and used all 315 hp to get off the ground at about 7:30 am, headed for Galena 220 miles away. The plane felt stable and easily trimmed out and flew straight. Josh was only a couple of hundred pounds over gross which was about normal for most Cessnas flying in the Alaskan bush. Angel really liked the 206: it was so quiet and the vibration was so much less than the 185. She slept for an hour, almost all the way to Galena.

They overflew Galena, turned toward Hughes, and flew at less than 1000 AGL. Angel knew they changed headings, and seemed to be paying attention to the scenery now. She liked flying low: there was a lot to see and sniff: life was good in the new plane.

Landing at Hughes, the 206 was still a little over gross, Josh did his best to smooth it in. Angel hardly felt the landing but wasn't comforted by the squeal of the tires; she still remembered the last landing at Bettles. Before Angel was allowed out of the plane, she had to undergo the shame of a leash: she hated a leash. A leash was for dogs too stupid to stay out of trouble: not for Angel.

After they walked off the ramp, the leash came off and she ran to find a bush to claim. Josh found a tree near a picnic table and they shared some jerky, while Josh drank a Coke. Angel did not like Coke, not at all. She preferred a nice cloudy puddle of water if one was available. While they sat at Hughes airstrip there was no other air traffic, none at all.

They spent an hour there before taking off again, this time to the north east. Another new direction, Angel thought: was he lost or what?

After Hughes they crossed over the Brooks Range, heading to the Coleville, another 185 miles. Josh decided to keep it low, less than 700 feet elevation, till he landed at the river airstrip.

He was sure he'd find it from the lower elevation and, if not, he could easily climb a little for a look-see. The strip was on the 36 degree radial of the Dead Horse VOR: about 215 miles west south west. He knew if he was over the river on that radial he could easily find his way.

126

Up and over the Brooks Range is really not very up. The mountains along his route top out at 4800 feet, hardly tall mountains: the air was stable and very clean. Josh crossed the north south divide at an angle, maybe 45 degrees, and 6,000 feet at 155 knots. Dropping the nose a little, they got up to 180 knots for awhile: the air was smooth and they were flying!

As the slope of the land levelled out, a few low clouds formed and the ceiling went from about 9,000 feet to 800 feet in less than 50 miles. Josh found what he thought was the Colville River and followed it north east looking for the strip. He continued flying; farther, much farther than he thought he should, with no luck. He was just about to turn back, when he over flew the village of Umiat and its air strip. He'd gone just 25 miles too far. Josh wasn't lost; but he didn't know where he was. As he made the 180 turn, he saw a familiar looking Super Cub parked next to the runway and next to the Cub, a Mooney 201, and Bud Hastings's silver Cessna 170. Bud's 170 had a 180 hp engine conversion, which made it a pretty good performer. Bud really liked Cessna 170's.

Josh had seen the Mooney before: there weren't that many Mooney around. They were distinctive with their proud vertical tail. They hadn't followed him today, maybe because they knew where he was going. Or maybe it was nothing but coincidence: after all, what's so strange about two aircraft crossing paths while randomly flying over half a million square miles of Alaskan wilderness?

On the way back Josh would need to refuel at Bettles and then, if the weather holds, he'd be back to the Valley by evening. The total trip is 900 miles and about 6 hours of flight time depending on the winds. The big difference between this trip and the last was that this time he kept off the radio, totally. He wasn't talking to flight Services and planned to give a phony tail fin number if he found he had to use the radio. He knew Kevin's tail number, his friend at Bettles, and he would use it if necessary, anywhere close to Bettles.

It took Josh 25 minutes to find the air strip near the strip mine. The landing was a little long and he had to turn around and back taxi to the ramp. The 206 is such an easy plane to operate, he wondered why he'd ever had a 185 to begin with. He knew the answer, as he was thinking up the question: they are two different planes with two different missions.

While parking the plane the larger of the two Indians that he'd seen before and a helper pulled a trailer out to the plane with a 4 wheeler. Josh had the cargo door open and was standing back, watching cases of booze get unloaded. He started to help but the Indian waved him off in a friendly manner. Josh brought out the lock box and the cardboard box with the gloves and such, and told Angel to be still until the cargo was off and away from the plane. Angel was not happy: she was still harnessed while everyone else was busy doing their thing. She wanted to supervise the goings on and was not even allowed to get out of the plane. This could've been handled better and if it continues I will stay home next time: fat chance!

The Indian said, "I have seen you before of course but we have never been introduced, my name is Hector Redhorse. I work here as a Construction Foreman and I handle security issues as they come up. Welcome to our discovery project!"

Josh: "Hector, my name is Josh Browning; I own the Golden Valley General store in Goldstream Valley just outside of Fairbanks. I'm pleased to meet you. Today I'm the Goldstream Air Services chief delivery pilot"

They shook hands and Hector noticed Angel and asked if he could talk to her. "Yes, of course. I'll take her out of her harness if it's Ok with you that she runs loose. She is very well behaved and won't roam farther than she can hear."

Hector: "Yes, of course, let her run."

Josh reached over the seat and took Angel's harness off. She bounded over the seat and jumped out of the cargo door instead of going out the pilot's door.

Hector: "There are no other dogs around except for our

Border collie and he is in the office now."

After talking to Angel, giving great ear rubs, and getting a friendly hand lick, Hector said, "What a fine dog you have. If she ever has a litter I would pay well for a pup from her, and if ever I get the chance, I would promise to take very good care of it and never hook the pup up to a sled."

Josh said if that ever happened he would contact Hector but he had no plans to breed her.

He said, "She is really very well behaved. The only time I have trouble with her is when she is in heat. I guess that's true with most any animal." Josh refused to refer to Angel as a bitch.

Hector said, "It would be a shame to end the blood line of an obviously intelligent and healthy animal, I hope you re-consider sometime."

Angel did not understand the words but somehow knew she was the target of the conversation: She felt very important and wondered if treats would be coming her way.

Hector then walked the lock box back to the shed and came back with his payment, which Josh counted as the Indian watched. The money was complete. When Josh said he'd be leaving, he was asked, if he'd take another package back to the store where it would be picked up in the morning by Carter. Josh agreed and visited another tree next to the strip, had a Coke, and waited for the package. Angel ran around and chased a Parka squirrel up a small aspen. She usually felt good and in charge after asserting her authority over a squirrel, or even better another dog. She wondered where the other dog was: his scent was all over the place.

Josh gave her a jerky strip and he had one also. He planned to eat at the lodge in Bettles when stopping to fuel the plane. He would buy Kevin Ferguson lunch too, if he was around. Josh wanted to ask if Kevin had seen the Mooney or the Super Cub in the last week. Kevin would be surprised to see the 206.

Hector came out of the shack carrying the lock box, and

followed by a beautiful black and white Border collie. Angel and the Collie sniffed butts, wagged, and were instant friends. They tried to romp off, but Josh and Hector both told them to cool it and come back.

Hector asked Josh to be careful with the box: he asked Josh to lock it up until Carter came to the store. Josh promised. It turned out to be an empty promise: almost. Josh strapped the box down behind the pilot's seat and shook hands with Hector again. Josh and Angel both said goodbye to Charlie the Collie and then Josh said "Kennel up, Angel!" She jumped into the plane and sat quietly in the Co-pilot's seat as Josh put on her harness.

Josh: "See you on the next trip, Hector. I hope there is another trip. Take care"

Hector: "Take care of yourself, Josh, and listen to Angel, she has good insight." Angel wagged and was proud: they were talking about her again and she liked the attention.

Hector had been pleasant to Josh and very nice to Angel. Angel seemed to like him and Josh knew that Angel had a knack of identifying friend or foe with a degree of accuracy.

At a distance, Hector looked like a big man. Up close he was huge: 6'5", maybe a little taller, perhaps 245 pounds or so, but he moved like a dancer. Hector seemed intelligent and well educated. Josh hoped if there were ever problems he and Hector would be on the same side.

Before takeoff Josh checked his oil and rechecked his total fuel. He had less than he planned on. There were good tail winds on the trip north but by overshooting the airstrip all the way to Umiat and back, he used more fuel than expected and would need fuel at Bettles, for sure, which was another 140 miles. Josh was unsure how much fuel the 206 used: he knew what the manual said it should use but he needed some history before he could try to stretch the limits.

Low fuel and no cargo let the 206 get airborne in just a few hundred feet. Nothing of interest happened on the way to

Bettles. After crossing the north south divide of the Brooks Range, Josh set the autopilot for 155 degrees and found a tail wind at 4500 feet. He relaxed. An hour later he was on short final for 19 at Bettles, it was wind calm, and he greased it in. Kevin was working in his hanger and very surprised to see Josh in a 206.

Kevin: "What did you do with your new tires and the plane that was attached to them?"

Josh: "I had some control cable issues and had to let the plane go three days ago. Sold it to a wannabe Bush Pilot: a real Bush Pilot now with a real Bush Pilot's Airplane."

Kevin: "Bud's new Assistant Guide?"

Josh: "That's the one. How did you know?"

Kevin: "Bud came by yesterday and told me about the trade but he didn't know it was you who got the 206 Bud was in a fairly new Mooney, have you seen it?"

Josh: "It was at Umiat earlier today. Is Bud's strip at his base camp cabins long enough for a Mooney?"

Kevin: "I don't know but I don't think so. Who'd want to fly a Mooney into that mud hole anyway? That suits his 170 better. He was probably dragging some clients up to Umiat and will most likely have one of his boys fly them from there to his cabins in his 170. Bud has done that before. He has a stopover sleeping facility at the strip at Umiat, I thought you knew that."

"I haven't paid much attention to the hunting seasons lately, with the store and all. I guess his clients are looking for Brown Bears now?"

"Yes, I think so, and maybe a Moose, maybe a Caribou: there are thousands in the local herd."

Kevin: "Last season Bud brought me an almost complete bull that went over 300 pounds dressed out. Said the client didn't want it, only wanted the antlers. Molly and I are still eating on it. It makes great sausage, you know."

Josh: "Yes I know, you gave Claire ten pounds of it. We have it with noodles now and again. Ain't freezers wonderful?"

Josh only bought 40 gallons of fuel. He was not hungry for dinner now, for wondering about Bud's involvement, and wanting to get back to the valley quickly to talk to Skip. What were hoods from Fargo doing with an Alaska Master Guide? Nothing made real sense. Josh hoped Bud wasn't involved beyond transportation. Bud had once been a real close friend.

Josh, uptight, was barely able to pre-flight the plane. He had to use his check list for the first time in, well, almost forever. He and Angel both had two more strips of jerky and Josh drank one more Coke. Angel found a puddle and a friendly aspen tree. Josh turned down the lunch invitation and almost left without paying for the fuel. Kevin reminded him by producing his new Credit Card reader.

Late in the afternoon after an hour fifteen minute flight Josh landed the 206 behind the store in Goldstream Valley. He locked up the plane, then locked the cash payment in the gun safe. He was still preoccupied and barely spoke to Claire. He called Skip on the phone. Skip was not at his restaurant/lounge in Fairbanks. Josh left a message for him to please call.

Claire: "It's nice to see you too, but please don't waste my time with small talk."

Josh: "Sorry, kid, But I don't have a clue what the hell is going on. If I don't get some answers we're getting out of the booze delivery business. This lock box I've been delivering is a puzzle. I just weighed it and it weighs exactly the same as when I took it north. Not only that, it hasn't been opened. I set a marker. Why the hell have I been flying around a locked box? I have to see Skip; if I knew where he was I'd go there now."

Claire: "Skip is next store at the Exchange: why didn't you ask? Better calm down, you're ripe for a stroke, fly boy."

Josh: "I'm going next door. Angel stay!"

Tommy was giving Skip a pool lesson. He was down $6.00 and ready to lose another buck, with a shot that he forgot to call. Tommy was beaming: he loved to win Skip's money. Josh had been in overdrive since Bettles, and he was in no mood to

132

get slowed down by a game of pool. He asked Skip to come over to the store for a few minutes.

Skip: "I'll be there in two minutes, as soon as I finish contributing to the Don and Tommy Retirement Fund."

Tommy "Why is it always Don and Tommy? Why is it never Tommy and Don? I count too, you know, I do, I am at least half of this operation and pretty much considered boss. If anyone thinks differently, just ask Don!"

Don walked in from the kitchen drinking a glass of wine.

Tommy asked, "Don, who's the boss around here: you or me? Do you like that new White Zinfandel? I hope you do, I just bought six cases, I know I should have asked first, but you were nowhere to be found."

Don: "Whatever."

# CHAPTER TWENTY-ONE

## — THE MYSTERY: FINALLY REVEALED —

WHEN SKIP arrived at the store, Josh had the lock box in the back room and his tool box out. He asked Skip if he'd pick the lock but before Skip could use one of his many talents, they heard Claire saying Hi to Carter out front. Josh quickly put the tool box away and started talking about the new 206, and how well it went today. Carter wandered back and politely listened to Josh brag about how well the plane flew and all those pilot things that he knew little about. After a while Carter asked about the lock box and Josh picked it off a shelf and handed it to him.

Carter: "I bet you want to know what you're bringing me."

Josh: "I am curious, yes"

Carter: "I have a key. Let's open it now."

Skip turned to leave but Carter said: "It's OK, Skip, you can see it also. It's my guess that you know more than you're willing to say and after today, this'll be no secret anymore. We just yesterday completed the leases on the land and are ready to start this operation for real."

Josh: "What operation?"

Skip: "Diamonds, real diamonds. You guys are mining and sluicing diamonds?"

Carter: "Yes, Skip, you're right, real diamonds. It's a long story, but I bet you'd like to know so I won't shorten it."

Carter: "The original oil exploration companies defining the length and breadth of the Prudhoe Bay oil field drilled a bunch of other test wells on the North Slope. Two of the wells west of the main field were near where Josh delivered the whiskey. The wells weren't totally dry of oil but gushers they aren't: at least they would not be profitable. But the material surfacing from the drilling seemed to be a kimberlitic material, not shale as you might expect. The Kimberlite was familiar to one of the drillers because he'd worked in South Africa for

De Beers. He recognized the drilling residue. Excited, he told the Geologist they had kimberlite tailings and there might be diamonds in the area, but the Geologist said they were in the oil business, not chasing rainbows. The Geologist did record it but thought the driller was smoking something: basically he thought nothing of it. One of my security managers heard about the kimberlite tailings at a bar one night and after many weeks and many drillers, he finally found the right driller and bought the information: the bore location and number. My security manager found and copied the drilling logs of that bore. He had access to the offices at night, so it was easy to get once he knew which well was the one. The data confirmed the tailings were kimberlite, as the driller said. We thought it might be worth a look see, so we hired an independent Geologist and paid Bud Hastings to fly him around the area. Bud had flown for the exploration companies and was very familiar with the drill sites. Just because you find a little kimberlitic material doesn't mean you find diamonds of value though, you may or you may not, but it does mean you should have a look. Our Geologist found enough to allow us to get financing to go as far as we have. We now, as of yesterday, have the leases signed and paid for. It's a go as soon as the checks hit the bank and the leases hit the recorder's office. We're no longer just a security consulting agency; we're officially a Mineral Exploration and Development Company. Now don't spread it around but everything really looks good."

Carter pulled a key from his pocket and put it in the lock. He turned the key, opened the lid of the box, and took out a blue cloth zippered bag with two dozen stones. They looked much like quartz but weren't. The stones were noticeably heavier than quartz, but other than that they were unremarkable. "This is the find for the last week or so: pretty handsome don't you think?"

Josh: "Sure, but I don't get the whiskey deliveries, what's the deal with a dozen pallets of liter bottles of R&R Canadian

Rye whiskey? What is going on there?"

Carter: "Not much. Hector is selling the booze, like I told you when you started two months ago. Hector manages the site and handles the entire logistics. He's making a lot of money for himself but he's breaking no laws. I don't think he would just for a few more bucks. Hector is a pretty bright guy. But much more important, it is, or rather was, the cover story for our little diamond exploration strip mine."

Carter went on: "We did have a serious problem a while ago. It involved the shooting of a helper. One of Hector's guys, he got shot in the leg and his river boat was destroyed by two wise guy hoods from Fargo. They don't think Hector should be supplying whiskey on the Slope. They think they can dictate who gets to sell and who doesn't, that they can push vendors out of a market place, much like the drug sellers might do on the street corners in the big cities. You were there that day and saw the boat. These guys might have been looking for you but they found Sam, Hector's helper, and tried to bully him and his boat off the river. If they'd found you, my guess is they'd have punched you around a little and destroyed your plane. The fact is, Sam was minding his business waiting for your delivery when a Super Cub landed with two guys in it. Sam, being friendly, started a friendly conversation. These guys were not friendly. When Sam went for his rifle, the younger of the two guys grabbed it away and shot up his boat, his personal boat; you saw it on the gravel bar. Sam is not a rich man and his boat is a big part of his personal wealth. He's not timid like a lot of the locals and got kind of pissed and wouldn't back down. So there was a pushing contest, and one of the jerks fired a warning shot into the gravel. The damn fool hit Sam with a ricochet in his calf just below the knee. Sam bled like a stuck pig, so they figured the message had been delivered and they left, flew off downstream in their Cub, probably to their camp a little north of Umiat. The big camp there caters to tourist operations, fly ins and such, all the way from the lower 48, so

136

those guys kind of fit in with the other visitors. The tourist operations in the 'Gates of the Arctic' bring in quite a few people to enjoy a week of fishing and hiking: you know, living in the Bush."

Carter continued, "Anyway, Sam grabbed and tied up a couple of logs and managed to float down river far enough to reach us on his VHF radio. Luckily we have two jet boats so we picked him up in one and used the other to pick up the whiskey from you, which is why we were late. He's recovering a little more every day but still can't walk well. It's lucky he didn't bleed to death. Sam said the rifle shot was an accident: he thinks the thugs were just bullies trying to push around a timid Indian. He didn't want the police involved, so we left it at that, but Hector went to visit the manager of the camp where the wise guys are staying, to make new policy: tourist customers stay north of Umiat now. The manager of the camp is still recovering from his conversation with Hector. The camp manager recognized the error in his ways, he's a very generous person. Since Sam didn't file a police action he bought him a new jet boat and a new rifle and scope. Sam's happy about the boat but prefers a flat bottom and is looking to make a trade." That's pretty much the story, but we will need air support for people and material in the coming months. We want the camp to support twelve people on a working basis in the summer and four during the winter months."

Josh: "I don't fly people, I'm not an Air Taxi Service but the folks here, at Grizzly Air, will be happy to handle people moving for you. Their equipment is well kept and safe. I'd like to continue to supply your cargo needs. I think by now you know that I do what I say when I say I will, right?"

Carter: "Yes, you have not made even one little screw up yet, you even purchased a new plane when the one you had was no longer serviceable. And you did it on your own without any assistance from us, though we did offer. We want you to keep flying for us, if we can set up a routine delivery schedule."

Josh: "I'm sure we can."

Josh: "Littlejohn had a bee in his bonnet last week: what does that donkey and his simpleton son, have to do with your operation, exactly. Was he the pilot of the Cub that landed on the Gravel bar?"

Carter: "Last question first. "Yes, we're quite positive he and his son were in the Cub. We're not sure what he wants regarding our diamond operation. And, Hector does not push drugs: you can believe that! As for Jim Littlejohn, he's a low level hood from Fargo, North Dakota, who pushes most, or at least some, of the drugs consumed on the North Slope. I guess, he thinks he has the booze distribution franchise also. Somehow or another he wants to hook up with the Teamsters but, from what my contacts tell me, they want nothing to do with him. I'm just guessing, but once he got information that you were transporting liquor he thought we were his competition. Which means, he and his son are folks not to be ignored: they are dangerous and not predictable. If I were you I'd stay away if possible. My guess is they sabotaged your 185."

Josh: "Seems likely. I saw their Super Cub in Umiat today. Do you have any idea why the plane was there?

Carter: "Don't know but maybe Umiat is part of their drug pipeline. I know they tried to hire Bud Hastings to fly a few hundred pounds of something into Deadhorse a few weeks ago and he turned them down. Bud said he was a Guide, not a pharmacy. They quietly backed away: I think because Bud has too many people to back him up. You'd know better than I."

Skip was inspecting the raw stones.

Josh thought "Is he a diamond expert too?"

A sudden ruckus in the store stopped the conversation. Josh went to investigate. Claire was in a heated discussion with someone in an animal control uniform who was trying to hook up Angel to a control collar. Angel wasn't cooperating at all. Claire was ready to commit mayhem.

Josh: "What the hell is going on here?"

Clark: "I'm Clark Richards from Borough Animal Control and I'm taking this dog for observation: she may have rabies.

Josh: "Well Clark, my name is Josh and the lady you are arguing with is my wife Claire. We own this store and this is our guard dog Angel. You will not be taking 'Michel's Angel of Jordon' anywhere. Angel does not have rabies and I will thank you to take your little animal control collar and your little green uniform out of this store."

Clark: "You think you can throw me out? I'm a duly deputized officer of the law. You can't speak to me that way"

Skip: "Gentlemen, gentlemen, let's not get off on the wrong foot. Let's talk this problem out. Clark, what's in the nature of your belief that Angel has rabies?"

Clark: "She bit David Littlejohn and he is undergoing a series of rabies shots, so she must be quarantined."

Josh: "Why?"

Clark: "Because that is the law"

Josh: "That's not the law, that's just a regulation: I know the law. The animal must be quarantined if there is reasonable cause to believe the animal has rabies. That's the law. Angel does not have rabies. She was protecting Claire, my wife, from an assault perpetrated by Jim littlejohn. And if you press this phony action against Angel, I will file an action against you, David Littlejohn and his father, who's the person that assaulted my wife, before Angel protected her. Are you by chance a friend of David?"

Clarke: "Not a friend but I know him, yes."

Josh "Does that give you comfort, to know that you are doing the right thing?"

Clark: "I see your point. I'll take this to my supervisor. You will be hearing from him. I'm an officer of the law and you'll have to release that dangerous dog to my custody then."

Jean entered the conversation: "Not even the smallest chance you'll ever take Angel, not the least chance in hell."

Poor Clark, outnumbered and unsure of what to do next,

did what he had to do: he left the store and drove away.

Carter stayed in the back of the store and heard most of the argument. At one point he almost added an opinion, but decided he wasn't needed. Skip was ready for a drink. Josh asked him to stay for a few minutes and look at the plane.

Carter said it was late and he'd be getting back to his hotel for a Surf and Turf dinner. "Expense accounts are great."

Josh said it was kind of like stealing from one pocket and stuffing the other. Skip reminded him, it was deductible so you were really stealing from everyone, not just yourself.

Carter again suggested that Littlejohn and son were un-good and should be avoided. "I'm flying back to the Coleville tomorrow morning with Bud. I will see you later."

With Carter gone, Josh told Skip the real reason he wanted him to stay and talk: the lock box had not been opened between the time the box left the store in the morning and the time it came back. Whatever was in the box didn't come from the Colville River, at least not on this trip, which reminded Josh of the conversation he had with Earl Pilgrim. Earl had said, "Though people have found diamonds in many places in Alaska none have been profitable to mine, none!"

Skip asked Josh if he was absolutely positively sure of that the box hadn't been opened. Josh told him about the black pepper he had pressed into the space between the tumbler and the lock body.

Josh and Skip were thinking the same thing and they started to giggle, then laugh, and then started to roar. Claire and Jean came running to the back room to see if there was a fight going on, or something. Even Angel seemed to be having fun. Jean asked, "What the heck is going on?"

Skip: "Something really clever, Jean, something so cool that, well hell, we have to figure out what to do next. This is going to be unbelievable, really unbelievable!"

Claire: "Don't be so damn clever. What is going on?"

Josh: "We think Mr. Carter Thomas is greasing up the

Littlejohn boys for the biggest screwing of their lives. I love it!"

Claire: "I don't get it."

Skip: "Carter has a first class scam going, and he most likely has Jim Littlejohn believing there are diamonds on the Coleville River. I think, Littlejohn will be try to get control of the property somehow or another. Wonder how he will do it?"

Josh: "Something to do with controlling the mineral or oil leases is my bet. I guess we will see. I think we should back off of anything but flying in booze, and be careful not to piss anyone off."

Claire: "I will not be nice to little David, I will not."

Jean: "I agree, he is a jerk."

Skip: "Ok, but see if you can keep Angel out of the mix, she might get hurt and she does not deserve any more grief."

Josh: "Agreed, but let's just keep this among the four of us for now."

## Chapter Twenty-Two

### — What Next Diamond Miners? —

JOSH AND CLAIRE decided to dine in style at the Ivory Exchange as soon as they closed the store for the day. Jean had Casey working like a veteran, and Claire was close to current with the paper work.

Casey packed the fire boxes and turned out a half dozen now quicker than Claire could have. Josh did a quick delivery trip into Fairbanks and was off the clock for the night.

Claire invited Casey to join them for dinner. She accepted the invite. They'd known Casey for less than a week but already she seemed like part of their extended family group. For her part Casey seemed to need to be a part of a larger group: she seemed to want family.

Josh and Angel had eaten jerky for lunch and nothing more since then: they were hungry. Angel lucked out as she was presented with two more hunks of jerky and a good size bowl of Iams pet food. Angel really liked Iams but hoped for a steak bone when the folks got back from dinner.

Skip called Martha and she drove out to the Valley to join Skip, Josh, Claire, and Casey. Jean was also invited to the feed, but turned it down because she said she had a date. Josh thought, probably for the weekend because she had the next three days off.

Josh believed Jean might be part machine. She seemed straight laced and had no recognizable sense of humor. For her part, Jean was still waiting, saving her laughter, for a time that Josh might actually say or do something funny. It was a bit of a standoff but they did respect and thought fondly of each other: it was just that neither would say it, and why should they, as it was so perfect the way it was. Josh saw that Jean was totally honest and trustworthy and to him that was most important. Jean pretended to just tolerate Josh, but in fact she felt protected and safe in the store, and very much needed protection. The store and her extended family at the store walled off the part of her life she chose to leave: to forget.

Josh decided to pick up the dinner check. Skip insisted on paying for the drinks. Dinner was good as usual and in the late evening all the diners could hear was the clicking of pool balls from the lounge and a few darts hitting the board in the bar area. Soft music of the 50s filtering through the building. The evening was soft and lazy and almost romantic. Casey left, and said she would be in for work tomorrow on time and thank you for dinner.

Skip, Josh, and Claire had agreed earlier not to discuss the diamond mining scam with any one: not anyone. But there was a little more to be discussed between them. As it turned out, Skip had been offered, for a mere $100,000, a small part of a "dynamite investment". Jim Littlejohn made the proposal a few days ago when he just happened to have lunch at the Gold Bar. Skip asked if it was a gold mine and Jim said:"Even better than a gold mine, because this one can't miss! I need 2 million for lease options and we will be "in like Flynn". You in or out, for 5%."

Skip pretended to consider it and then said, "Out."

He claimed to have no free money at the time but was sure he smelled a rat. That was the day he warned Josh but at the time, well, Josh didn't know what to think. He just took the warning at face value and decided he'd think twice before extending any credit to the folks from Fargo, North Dakota.

Skip had trouble with the offer because he also knew about Jim Littlejohn's involvement with drugs distribution on the Slope, but in that venture Jim was just a minor player, a Lieutenant. Jim wanted to be a General, a Principle Player. Skip wondered what else Littlejohn and his kid were involved in that the rest of the Cartel wasn't aware of. Skip guessed that the Cartel knew nothing about the Diamond exploration and Littlejohn did not want them as partners in it. Skip decided to stay away, at arm's length, but to keep his ears open.

Josh and Skip had a long and close attachment. Martha and Skip were getting closer and Martha was developing a friendship with Claire, which seemed a good thing, because keeping secrets from one or another and having different degrees of trust within the group was bad. Skip and Josh had a separate sit down and decided to tell Martha and Claire all of what they suspected was going on. Claire already knew, more than Skip probably, but just the same she listened and nodded her head at the right time.

At first Martha wasn't able to see the humor in the situation but after she found out more about the players she began to enjoy it more. It was obvious to all that the thing to do was to do nothing: just sit back and watch. They agreed that none of them would try to make a buck on the scam, except that Josh would continue to fly whiskey or any other legal cargo up to the Coleville, as long as Carter paid him to.

Josh guessed that the booze transport business wouldn't last much longer. He saw that the whiskey deliveries were designed to be high profile, to attract the attention of Jim Littlejohn, so Littlejohn would discover the mining effort and try to gain control of what he thought would be a real money maker.

Angel pushed her way through the double doors and into the Ivory Exchange, walking right past the sign that said: No Dogs allowed except "Michel's Angel of Jordon" and "Yukon King". Angel was smart but she couldn't read, at least she couldn't read Human. She was there to tell the Kids, Josh and Claire, that it was time to come home and go to sleep. They might not know how to tell time but she sure as hell did her way!

Tommy walked out of the kitchen and handed Claire a bag with steak bones in it. "For Angel, if you don't mind."

Angel heard her name and knew what was happening: she liked Tommy a lot and walked to him for an ear rub.

Claire thanked Tommy and headed out the big double doors, followed by Josh still holding a glass of wine. He turned to Tommy to say, he'd bring it back tomorrow. Tommy said, "OK, but only if it's in one piece and clean."

Josh and Claire headed up the back steps and Josh kind of brushed Claire's bottom with the back of his hand. She turned and kissed him and then continued up the steps. Angel thought "There they go again."

A while later as they lay next to one another catching their breath, and just as Josh was about to nod off, Claire began laughing. Josh opened his eyes asked, "What's so funny?"

Claire: "You still have your socks on. Good night, Superman!"

## CHAPTER TWENTY-THREE

### — LIFE AT THE GOLDEN VALLEY STORE —

SATURDAY MORNING the store opened as it usually did at 9:00, but Soapies was already flush with customers. The folks that muck out the laundromat every morning don't lock up when they leave around 7:00. That lets the laundry folks get a head start on the day: after all, many people in the Valley work during the week. Two Maytag washers had given up the ghost and replacements had arrived Thursday afternoon. Jean had the delivery boys put them in the laundromat next to the new video machines, which made the store two hundred extra a month: who's to complain?

The washer installation was just R&R (rip out and replace). One new washer wouldn't take the tokens properly but a little work with a rat tail file got it friendly. Josh put water filters in the hot water lines and in less than an hour they were flowing money into the store. Josh started a log book on the machines to determine the ones with the most trouble but he was less than diligent keeping it up to date: a man is either a pilot or a book keeper, seldom competent at both tasks. It requires a different set of disciplines to do the mundane tasks in life: Josh was not mundane.

He thought, if you were bad in a previous life and came back to this world after death, you might be either a washing machine in a laundromat or a slot machine in a Casino. Neither of these machines ever quite lives up to the hopes and dreams of the users, and while they perform as expected they seldom perform as desired: or get much praise. Jean heard him say that once and just shook her head. A philosopher he isn't.

With the chores at Soapies complete, Josh counted the change taken in during the week. The pennies, nickels, and dimes came out about even week to week, but the quarters grew in numbers beyond belief. Canadian coins were accepted at the Golden Valley Store at face value even though they were

146

worth only 90 cents to the dollar. This made Canadian quarters worth 22.5 cents, and Canadian dimes worth 9 cents at the Bank of the North: a small but real problem for the bank. Josh sorted the Canadian coins to one bag and the "Human" coins to another. He also kept a bag for silver coins that hit the register. The bank had a coin counter to make the task easier, but it couldn't distinguish between Canadian and American.

Later in the day Josh and Casey put together eight more food boxes for the Rosie Creek fire fighters. Casey delivered them to the Department of Natural Recourses on University Avenue. She actually liked the work and was quite good at it. Josh thought: "Imagine a Doctoral candidate finding a general store interesting."

The "Bowzer Van", as Claire called it, a 30 ft trailer filled to the limit with dry dog food, was due Monday, tomorrow morning. Twice a year Josh had 12 tons of 40 lb bags of dog food brought up from Seattle. He did a good business with the local dog mushers. He leased the trailers and stored the dry food in the same van it was delivered in. If he could keep the mice and voles out he'd make a fair profit, even while offering a discount. As long as credit accounts were kept current on a monthly basis, he offered 5% off on fuel and dog food.

Dinner Sunday night was roast chicken and Tater Tots washed down with a mild white wine and apple pie for dessert. Angel didn't like Chicken Night: no bones for me tonight: sad!

Wrong! Claire had saved a steak bone that Tommy had given her. Angel wagged away.

Carter called late Sunday night and asked if Josh could fly in 24 cases of Whiskey and two cases of Single Malt Scotch, "The Glenlivet", 18 year old, one liter bottles and he'd stand a 50% markup on it. Josh, happy with that, said a Wednesday delivery was possible if the scotch was available in town. Carter said Pete would stop by early Wednesday with a box of "stuff" he also wanted flown in. He said Pete would pay for the R&R before the flight and he'd pay for the Glenlivet when delivered

147

as he didn't know the price. Josh said if the weight of the "extra stuff" was less than 150 lbs, it would go for free.

With the delivery business working out so well, Claire said, "We should have a Pow Wow on the future ownership of the store. The plane is ours, free and clear, but the Aviation side still owes the Store about $6,000. If you can charm Carter out of two more deliveries we'll be in Hog Heaven."

Josh: "Let's not forget we have the cable repairs on the 185 coming in, plus the cost of the Annual Inspection. I told Matt Smith we'd get him the plane in time for the fall season or he could use the 206: I don't want him flying the 206."

Claire: "With the money we've been making on the fire boxes we can handle the cable bill just fine. The repair expenses on the 185 is our personal responsibility, not the store's or the Aviation side. We weren't on Aviation time when those cables went democrat: we were on our own time. The Aviation business will pick up Annual inspection costs but only that."

Josh: "But I was —"

Claire cut him off. "You've no concept of Store billings, Aviation billings, or our personal expenses, do you? in fact I sleep pretty well lately thanks to your flying skills: and your socks. But I've nightmares just thinking that you might someday get control of the books. Josh just smiled and suggested they retire early.

Angel thought: What again?

Monday morning, before the doors to the Store opened, Angel supervised the driver as he backed the Bowzer Van into its parking place. Josh chocked the wheels while the driver unhitched the fifth wheel. He then pulled the tractor forward and parked while he collected his bonus: three bottles of R&R. The driver helped Josh drag a set of wooden steps over in front of the van and when they were secure he unlocked and opened the back doors and displayed 600 bags of Extra High Protein Delicious Pet Food: it said so right on the side of the bag. If Josh could keep the mice out of the van he'd have $2,400 in profit by the time it was empty. The store had been out of dog food for weeks and Josh had to buy some locally and resell it at no profit. Josh couldn't take the chance of losing customers by admitting he was out of food. Angel looked at the stash of food and wagged her tail: Life is good!

Josh had ordered the whiskey and scotch early from P&J but they couldn't deliver in time, so he did his own run. The pickup at P&J was easy: Josh just opened the side door on the van and it filled as if by magic, with the help of two guys who obviously had been sampling the merchandise. The two cases of single malt went on the front seat. The guy who loaded it said, if the scotch could be paid for in cash now, there'd be a big discount. Josh said absolutely no. No smiles there.

As Josh pulled away from the warehouse, he noticed a really puzzling thing. Pete, Carter's employee, and David Littlejohn, were sitting in a car together having a conversation and smoking weed. That meeting should not be going on, if Josh understood the situation correctly. Josh wondered if Pete was really trusted or just a stooge. He decided he'd mention it to Carter tomorrow: why would he not?

Back at the store he transferred the booze to the plane, strapped it down, and locked it up tight. He didn't plan to use the plane until Wednesday, but it was ready to go, full of gas, charts, a clean windshield, and a mission. He decided to name his new plane "Dexter": a good name for a hard worker.

With Josh so busy, Claire had a meeting with Jean and Casey, to decide whether to hire another helper, or did Jean and Casey want the extra hours? They decided to do with just the three of them, at least for the short term. Josh wondered why he was not invited to the meeting and Jean said it because "Nobody cared what he thought anyway."

That made sense to him so he popped a beer and sat on the swing on the front porch sipping it and chewing the jerky he found neatly packaged next to the cash register. Jean put a one dollar IOU chit in the cash drawer, with "JOSH" printed on it: the store's detective, what's her name, was sleeping under the swing and had missed the jerky theft.

Later, Josh, seeing Skip going into The Ivory Exchange, wandered over to visit and enjoy a beer. Josh wondered how much Skip had contributed to the Tommy Wilson Retirement Trust: via Tommy's pool skills.

Josh had his own trust to feed also. Tuesday was the day the liquor salesmen came to visit too. Josh had his wish list prepared, but asked about liquor sales anyway. He'd usually spend twenty bucks to save one. Claire never questioned or criticized his aircraft flying skills, nor did she ever compliment his liquor marketing skills. Jean was less kind and said, "When it comes to purchasing and inventory control in the liquor department, Josh is just dorky."

# Chapter Twenty-four

## — The Real Action Starts —

WEDNESDAY MORNING, Pete arrived at the store pretty early. He parked his car by the side of the building, not in back near the plane: he'd been warned. The store wasn't yet open and Josh was giving the water softener its daily feeding of salt. Angel was helping him and guarding the dozen forty pound bags of Iams pet food stored near the green bags of salt pellets. This was Angel's favorite place away from the hustle and bustle of the store. In the winter it was always warm, thanks to the boiler for the laundromat's hot water supply.

Also it had a pet door, a special kind that Angel knew how to open and that raccoons and the like would never be able to figure out: she hoped. The bags of Iams pet food were the stores reserve supply. Josh didn't want to run out again, and Angel could enjoy the expectation of them meanwhile.

While waiting for the softener to cycle through its back flush, Josh gave the 206 plane a good pre-flight inspection. He even checked the air pressure in the tires: they were fine.

Pete came walking around the corner carrying the extra stuff Carter wanted delivered. Angel all of a sudden seemed a little nervous. She wouldn't take her eyes off Pete and tried to stay between Pete and Josh. Pete put two of the extra items to be delivered near the cargo door but not in the plane. He knew that Josh and only Josh loaded his plane. Pete almost wouldn't let go of a file box of papers though and what looked like legal documents.

Josh noticed Pete was packing something under his jacket, probably a pistol, a small one by the size of the bulge. Side arms were not uncommon but Pete was getting twitchy: he seemed to be seriously up tight this morning. Josh wondered what the hell was in the file box and a brownish small zippered satchel. Actually he had a good idea what was in the satchel: it was the other box of papers that had his curiosity peaked.

Pete finally said his goodbyes to Josh and Angel and started to walk back toward his car, when David Littlejohn came around the corner of the Ivory Exchange with a rather large man and a very little 9 mm pistol in hand.

Pete froze as David said, "Give me that file box and satchel or you are a walking dead man! Tell your dog to sit, or stay, or whatever you say to her, or I will shoot both of you here and now."

Josh: "OK, OK. Angel, stay!"

Angel sat down but she sure as hell didn't want to.

Josh: "David, what the hell is going on? Are you sure you want to do whatever you're doing? You could get hurt David!"

David: "Just give those leases to Bob here and shut up!"

Josh: "OK, OK, they're on the dock: did you say leases?"

David: "Shut the hell up, Josh, and back off."

David told his buddy Bob to get the file box and satchel.

But before he could grab the file box, Claire came out and saw what was going on.

Claire: "What the hell? David, I told you never to come back here."

David pointed his gun at Claire. "I don't want trouble, just give me the leases and I'll be gone. Don't think I won't shoot. I will just as sure as I'm standing here."

Josh: "Claire, just stop. He only wants the files that I'm supposed to take north. Let's just give them to him and not get shot, or something. Don't do anything to get this prick upset. Sorry for the prick remark, Dave."

David: "My name is David, not Dave. Show some damn respect. I'm the one with the gun. Dammit Bob, get the box and satchel also. Where the heck is the satchel? Where'd it go? Where's that dammed dog?"

Bob: "The dog ran off with the satchel when that broad came out. I don't know where it went. He just grabbed the satchel and took off, I think toward the laundromat."

Claire: "Call me a broad again, you'll end up a eunuch."

152

Bob turned to Claire: "What's a eunuch?"

David: "Where did the dog go?"

Bob: "The dog ran that way" He pointed again to Soapies.

David: "Now where did the broad go? We got the leases, hell, that's what counts. Let's get out of here, Bob."

Josh: "What leases?"

David: "That's for me to know and you to —. Screw you Josh! Bob, let's go, I said, let's get the hell gone."

Pete: "You got nothing! Nothing but big trouble, big, big trouble!"

With that David and his big friend Bob walked backwards to a Jeep wagon parked next to the Ivory exchange and burned rubber out to the road.

Josh had never been robbed before; he was stunned, and kind of surprised, and really pissed. Pete was not all that excited and seemed to be calming down: he was almost smiling.

Pete: "OK now, that's over with. Can I ride up to the Coleville with you today? I got some important stuff to talk to Carter about, that shouldn't go over the satellite phone."

Josh: "What the hell are you talking about? In case you hadn't noticed, we just got robbed; I think we should call a cop, don't you?"

Pete: "No, god no, this is not police business. Carter will explain it to you. Really, so far so good. It's not what you think, really it's OK."

Josh: "What the hell are you talking about? For Christ sake, Pete, are you drunk or something? If you and Carter don't have a good explanation you'll walk back from the Coleville, got it? I have to put another seat in for Angel; I'll be just a few minutes."

Pete: "Where did Angel go with the Satchel?"

Josh: "Not a clue." Just then Angel came trotting around the corner of the building like nothing had happened.

Pete: "Where did she go and where is the satchel?

Josh: "Angel has a real fear of guns, sometimes she just

panics and runs away. I don't have a clue where to. Something to do with her police training, I think."

Pete: "We need that satchel, where did it go, where do you think it went?"

Josh :"I don't know, what was in it?"

Pete was now stumped. He didn't want Josh to know it was diamonds going north to the mining site instead of south, from the mine.

Pete: "It was just my lunch."

The seat meant nothing to Angel, but when she saw her harness she knew she was going and she was ready. Claire came quietly and slowly out the back door with her Mini 14. A little late, she thought: but just in case.

Claire: "I had a hell of a time finding the key for the gun safe. Why do you hide it so well? Josh, now just what the hell is happening?

Josh: "Ask Pete, he won't tell me much of anything"

Pete: "Can you put another seat in the plane for Carter? I think he might want to fly back today."

Josh: "Sure, whatever, I'm turning into a damn air taxi service. I hate hauling people!"

Claire: "Just a minute here, pal. Tell me what happened! You better have some real good explanations, mister. Never mind, just have a great day, Poop Head!"

Josh: "Poop Head? I haven't heard that one in a while."

Claire: "Come back safe, fly boy, both you and Angel."

And with that she turned and walked back into the store, Mini 14 in hand.

Josh: "That little prick David came within two minutes of getting really fucked up. Claire would have shot him; she'd really have shot him, trust me, she would without blinking an eye, if she thought one of us was in danger."

Pete: "That was a close one. When can we leave?"

Josh: "I need a donut and a cup of decaf coffee, want one?"

Josh, Pete, and Angel took off at 9:30 after mandatory

bathroom visits and a final sarcastic "so long" from Claire who had not cooled down even one little bit. She did, however, promise to not kill any paying customers for the rest of the day, unless it was either father or son Littlejohn.

Josh told her confidentially, it was more complicated than they had thought, but Skip was at least partially correct that there probably were no diamonds of great or even moderate value on the Coleville River. Claire said, it was her professional opinion, as a State of Alaska Registered Geologist, that she did not know and had no opinion: then she smiled ear to ear.

Claire had a sense of humor that Josh had always envied, and while he didn't always understand what she was thinking, he was usually, almost always pleased with her demeanor and her attitude toward life. She could find humor in most any situation and not lose track of reality. He really loved her and the feeling was mutual: Claire had no intention of seeing Josh go off into a dangerous situation, but she knew that the danger was probably in and around Fairbanks: where ever the Littlejohn group was. Claire went up to the apartment again and opened the gun safe. She strapped on a five shot, nickel plated Colt Detective Special with a snub nose. She put on a loose fitting shirt and decided to share her concerns with Jean and Casey. Back down in the store she put the Mini 14 up on the top shelf, behind the cigarette case, next to the cash register. Claire was set for the day.

Before leaving and because of the added seats, Josh had to repack the cases of whiskey and tie them down, so the plane's weight and balance were within the proper limits. A pilot could overload a 206 by an unbelievable amount but every pilot knew to keep that balance within the "balance envelope", and the more the plane was overloaded, the better the balance had to be. The take off went smooth without incident.

Angel slept in her harness almost all the way. She could not see as well from the back seat and resented Pete for getting the best viewing spot. Angel wanted the front seat. They flew straight to the river with no problems, except Josh and Pete had to unload the plane themselves. Hector was not around and Carter was as much help with the whiskey cases as a box of rocks would be to a swimming contest.

Josh unshackled Angel and she ran around looking for a squirrel to chase. She also wondered where that other dog was. Pete and Carter talked for several minutes and then Carter told Josh what he had pretty much figured out on his own.

Jim Littlejohn had sent Carter's check back torn in pieces. It had been delivered a short while ago by two thugs in a boat from the Tourist Camp north of Umiat. They told Carter to get himself and his equipment off the site in three days or they would drive the equipment into the river. Carter said: "OK, you win; I'll be out of here in three." The check had been no good anyway, but they didn't know that.

Jim Littlejohn had called Carter over the satellite phone and laughed at him, telling him he'd already bought the leases from the Native Corporation. He bought them along with the options to purchase, that a small, almost bankrupt, oil company was struggling to buy. He bought them right out from under Carter's nose. Carter's check had been for $825,000. Littlejohn and his investors had upped the offer to $870,000 and paid for the leases. Since the option holders hadn't yet cashed Carter's check, they sold the options on the leases to the Littlejohn Cartel, instead of to Carter and his investors. Witlessly, Littlejohn bragged that everything was already recorded and locked up in a safe deposit box in Bank of the North. Basically he said Carter was screwed and should go back to his security business, and leave mineral exploration to the professionals.

Carter: "I asked if I could buy a small piece of the action and he laughed at me. He said I was a loser and have dinner with my loser friends in Goldstream and dream of what might have been. Then the bastard hung up and somehow charged the satellite call to my account."

Carter went on: "Littlejohn will hit the roof when he finds out that the Native corporation did own the leases but I owned the options to buy them: and they paid me through my shell corporation, the oil company. They paid me almost a million bucks for them. The oil leases were almost worthless. Hector got the options for little or nothing: Hector is no dummy! He is in for a great payday."

Carter continued: "I wanted to go back with you guys but I have to get this equipment back to Alyeska or pay more rent. A couple of Teamster foremen are renting the equipment to me and no, they don't own the Cat and Loader but they do control them. The rent was cheap. It cost me three pallets of R&R, about 4,300 gallons of fuel and a couple cases of Single Malt, now less one bottle.""Hector sold the rest of the booze in Deadhorse to attract and piss off Jim Littlejohn.

Carter had needed the whiskey sales to bring Jim Littlejohn to the false diamond mine just as Josh and Skip had guessed. The story about Hector was never even close to being believable. Josh was sorry to see the booze delivery business evaporating, but it had been good for a while and bought him a pretty nice plane.

Carter: "How close are you to paying off the new plane?"

Josh: "$10,000, we still had a very small note on the 185: actually we might have just paid it off, I'd have to check with Claire. If we include the cost of repairing the 185 it's probably around $12K. Again I would have to ask Claire."

Josh was sure the numbers he gave Carter were high but he thought he might at least try: Carter had just bragged he was almost a millionaire: so what the hell, go for it.

Carter "Did Pete pay you for the booze today?"

Pete: "No, I forgot to pay him in all the excitement this morning: I have the money here." Pete handed Josh an envelope with the usual hundred dollar bills in it.

Carter: "I am writing the store a check for $18,000 as a final payment to you and for your problems which we caused.

Also, for your help with this little swindle though you were kind of an innocent player."

Carter wrote Josh the check. He put it in his money clip and started to hum a tune of unknown verse. Carter scratched Angel's ears, as Pete opened one of the bottles of Glenlivet. Josh passed on it, since he was flying, but Pete sipped his share plus his own.

Pete: "David Littlejohn paid me four thou to set up the theft of the lease options this morning. Do you think I can keep a portion of it, Carter?"

Carter: "Pete, you can keep it all, pretend I don't even know about it."

Pete: "Carter, I don't think I told you, but Claire was within two minutes of shooting David this morning, it was a close one that we did not plan on."

Josh: "She would have too. Now that I know what really happened, I think it was lucky, she had trouble finding the key to the gun safe."

Carter: "I'll drink to that!"

Josh: "Pete, are you coming back to the Valley with me?"

Carter: "Would you mind taking Pete back? He needs a few days off"

Josh: "No that's fine, I planned on it. I brought a seat for you too."

Carter: "Pete, I've one more thing I want you to do before tomorrow."

Carter handed Pete a business card and asked him to call a number and tell whoever answered that things went well and he'd see them in a week's time.

Pete: "I could do that, my car is in the Valley and I have a few bills to pay and few to collect. I will make the call tonight."

With that and after a hand shake, they were off. Pete and Angel were Josh's only passengers on the way back, in the totally paid off, free and clear 206.

## CHAPTER TWENTY-FIVE

### — A TRIP TO THE WEST COAST —

THURSDAY MORNING Josh made a run to the bank to deposit the check he got from Carter. He knew that he'd made his last whiskey delivery to the Coleville River but thought there'd be other deliveries to other places. Alaska's a big State and tomorrow will bring what tomorrow will bring.

Claire thought the check generous and after some math decided they'd pay off the 206 debt to the store, then set up a sinking fund for the plane when needed. This'd also make a really big dent in the payments for the store. Josh thought such a fund should be called a floating fund instead of sinking since it would increase, not decrease: Claire just looked at him and shook her head.

Josh said "What?"

Josh noticed Claire's Colt under her shirt but was smart enough not to mention it. The 206 was parked and tied down behind the store. Angel rested on the back porch with one eye open and listened to the quiet of the valley. Occasionally a car drove by the store to break the solitude.

Grizzly Air service, the Air Taxi a hundred yards down the runway, had been quiet for a few days. One of the more senior pilots was busy changing the oil and washing the wings and tail section of their only 206. They'd been flying a few Fish and Wildlife folks around the Northern Region taking some counts on the 40 Mile Caribou Herd. The herd was about as far north as it could get and was almost done calving. Wolf packs, six of them, were doing their best but there was so much to eat and so little time. In just a few days or a week, a calf could outrun a wolf for a short distance and the cows, sometimes backed up by the bulls, were very aggressive to the predators. A bull Caribou is no soft target for a wolf, even a few of them. Such is the terror of nature! It's tough making a living as a wolf, but not this time of year.

The fire season was almost over. The same westerly winds that make the Interior a desert in the winter and keep it dry in the spring, bring rains in the summer. As soon as the Bering Strait is ice free, the westerly winds pick up moisture and bring rains to the Interior of the state. It mainly depends on how warm the spring and summer are, as to how much rain occurs, which kind of controls the length and severity of fire season.

The end of fire season meant less bucks coming in to the store but less goods going out, so the inventory of goods that only the firefighter's use had to be controlled tightly. Claire took that job on herself to make sure the shopping was for no more than needed. The crew now consisted of the three ladies, Josh, and one underpaid security expert, "Michaels Angel of Jordon", who guarded the underside of the front porch swing while recuperating from yet another flying ordeal perpetrated on her by "What's his name". Next time I get the front seat, or I ain't going!

With summer in full swing, tourists swarmed the town of Fairbanks and a goodly number make their way to the Goldstream Valley. The Ivory Exchange is a popular food stop for the visitors who don't depend on the tour companies for transportation but come by car or Motor Home. Some dinner folks will browse the Golden Valley Store's Native craft counter.

Claire applied the same profit margin on all of the store's Native crafts: 60% of the selling price of Native made crafts was gross profit. That markup made the quality merchandise a bargain compared to prices at tourist traps in the city. Smoke tanned moose hide moccasins, carved ivory, raw furs, whale bone and some soap stone carvings, were available at the Golden Valley Store for the best prices anywhere. These items were seldom available locally. It was Josh's burden to visit the villages and buy or trade craft items needed for resale.

Now that the store had a Cessna 206 Josh could haul a much larger load of "Trading Stuff", stuff always needed in the villages. He'd been planning a trip to Anaktuvuk Pass but was told that the Natives in the town were no longer making the Ceremonial masks so popular in the gift shops. Times were changing and the store would have to change with the times.

Josh made a decision, he decided not to visit the more out of the way villages but go instead to the larger towns to find new sources of Native arts and crafts from established businesses. On the trip he planned, he'd visit and do his ivory buying in the larger costal Eskimo towns on the west coast.

Josh had taken Angel on his last craft buying trip and in almost every village he'd been close to a dog fight. Angel would not back down when strange dogs challenged Josh. A couple of the Natives said that while Angel was a really nice dog maybe next visit Josh could leave her in Fairbanks. It did seem sage advice.

Josh wondered if Jean and Casey could handle the store for a week so Claire could join him on a trip to the bush. Jean said that with Josh gone that long the store would run better than ever: she told Claire that she and Casey were 100% up to the task. She didn't say that Casey had a friend who needed part time employment and wanted a chance to try out for a job, that Jean knew would be added soon. If push came to shove, they'd put a "Gone Moose Hunting" sign on the front door and close for a few days.

Jean: "Not to worry, just have a good time: with you as Navigator, "what's his name" might not get lost this time.

Jean was referring to a previous trip where Josh wasn't really lost: he just had no idea exactly where he was. He'd gotten a bit mixed up by setting his gyro compass 180 degrees off and, well, it was a little embarrassing. He'd been found, fed, and refueled, and everything came out OK. Since that time he had always responded to calls from the Civil Air Patrol Search and Rescue. Josh not only was a member but a firm supporter of the group. He didn't however attend meetings and knew if he ever did, he was sure he'd probably not salute as required. He really wasn't sure where meetings were held anyway. Somewhere at the airport, he thought.

Things were great in the Goldstream Valley in summer. Mid to high 80s weren't unusual and sales of beer singles sold steadily after 4:30 most any working day. Soapies was enjoying some of its best days for token sales, and the water softener had not gone democrat in two weeks time.

Tommy and Don from the Ivory Exchange came home on Saturday morning with a yellow Lab puppy they rescued from the Animal Control Center: Angel thought it was hers for awhile. The two of them became instant friends and Angel taught the little guy all about things a youngster should know: like to be careful when around people: they step on little paws. They named the little guy Spider, not a very good name for a dog, Angel thought, not very good indeed!

Josh and Claire prepared for the Native Craft buying trip. The only real plan was set by the places they'd land. The larger towns had restaurants and hotels, so they took a minimum of provisions. Since weather patterns on the coastal plains were not predictable, they planned to fly when they could and make the best of whatever happened. Being weathered in Nome would be inconvenient, but hardly life threatening. For emergencies, Claire put one large sleeping bag inside a very small rolled up tent stuffed with Snickers bars. There was the necessary saw, ax, single burner Coleman stove, frying pan, and a small pot to boil water, plus of course eight bottles of mosquito repellant. They took a single change of clothes and a toilet kit. That was about it.

Claire opened the safe and counted out five thousand dollars in hundreds, fifty's and twenty's. Checks were generally not accepted from non-residents, even in the larger towns.

Josh gave Jean a map of where they planned to go: it would be a way to start looking for the wreckage, if they were not back when planned. Casey would stay in the apartment and tend to Angel, who probably thought she'd tend to and protect Casey. Casey gave the best ear rubs of anyone, and

Angel wanted Casey to stick around the store always.

The 206 had long rang tanks, but when the tanks were three quarters empty you bought gas where ever you were, regardless of price: Claire's rule!

Josh had planned to visit Allakaket first, so Claire could meet the manager of the native corporation owned store and set up a mail order craft business. Josh had promised the manager he'd bring a craft buyer to the store and he always tried to keep his promises. Though Allakaket is a little north and out of the way, they'd make the trip anyway. After Allakaket they'd fly south-west to the west coast of the state.

Unalakleet is a fairly large town of 700 people located where the Unalakleet River runs into Norton Sound, well north of Bristol Bay. The airport has a 6,000 ft paved runway that handles small jets and a smaller 2,000 ft paved runway for smaller planes. The airport has fuel and a Fixed Base Operator (FBO) to handle airplane repairs. The town offers food and other services, even a lodge for the weary traveler to spend the night. Services not available would be done without, with grace and stealth, if necessary.

So that was the plan: go west as far as possible and buy Native artifacts and crafts until the money supply was gone and then fly home. Although Josh didn't mention it to Claire he also hoped to pick up a few collectable fire arms, if any were available. Might work, how hard can it be?

# CHAPTER TWENTY-SIX

## — CRAFT BUYING TRIP —

JOSH AND CLAIRE left Goldstream in the 206 on the following Sunday morning. Angel was sad to be left behind but would guard the store just as if they were there. She wondered how long they'd be gone, never questioning their return. Angel was very happy when Casey moved her duffle and sleeping bag up the stairs. Jean had been at the store the longest, so she got the most respect, but Casey gave the best ear rubs, and ear rubs are very important to a guard dog.

The first leg of the flight took them north west to Allakaket. The Native owned store manager was not in town so they left a message and advised they'd try to stop by on their return trip in a few days. From there, they took off: destination Unalakleet.

That flight took less than 2 hours. 260 miles go by fast in a lightly loaded 206. Josh wasn't wasting fuel. He had a nice easy cruise set up that ate the miles quickly. On this leg of the trip they'd also be looking for a supplier of legal Squaw Candy, that had the OK of the State Health and Welfare Department. There was a huge demand for the Candy in the Fairbanks area, but no legal suppliers that Josh was aware of.

Arriving in Unalakleet, Claire made a phone call to the local Native Corporation: Kawerak, to find information on who might have ivory and whale bone carvings available for the wholesale market. She came up the names of several artists with crafts to sell and the names of two more sellers in Nome, which was their next stop. The town was in walking distance of the airport so Josh and Claire grabbed their back packs and went to find lunch and a local artist or two. Lunch at the lodge was a Coke, an over-done hamburger, and over-done fries and what seemed like a week old green salad on the side.

Claire had gotten bad directions. That's fairly normal for Eskimos, but she still found the crafts suppliers. The carvings

164

offered were high quality and by the time she finished Claire's back pack was full and Josh had a fairly large cardboard box to carry back to the plane in addition to his pack. She and Josh bought just about everything shown for sale.

Josh also found a gun shop and bought a Trap Door Springfield rifle for next to nothing, and a 44 caliber Derringer, a real Derringer for $36. He also bought what Claire thought was a Remington painting of a couple of Cowboys and a mule train being attacked by a cougar. It was probably a fake but it only cost $18 and they liked it even so.

When dealing with the local artists, Natives in particular, Claire would stand a little behind Josh and jab him in the butt if she'd something to say. He'd then ask her what she thought and only then would she speak. According to Claire, Eskimos are very nice, maybe some of the very best people, but they have a culture of their own and the culture must be understood by people who interact with them. Eskimos are so eager to help that if an Eskimo is asked directions, they tend to give them according to what you hope to find, rather than what is real. If you ask about what they think the weather will be tomorrow they'll try to find out how you want the weather to be and tell you what you want to hear. Some people say Eskimos often lie for no apparent reason but others realize that culture, rather than guile, is the reason for the untruths.

Eskimos also have a strange sense of humor and absolute-ly no sense of political correctness. A man with a limp might be referred to as "gimpy", a man with one eye might be "light-house", and most any unfortunate happening to others will be recalled and reminded and laughed at forever. According to Josh, Eskimos just can't give directions; he claims to have no idea what this culture crap is that Claire's always talking about. Claire thinks Josh might be a highly disguised Republican.

Claire brought along a bunch of postal boxes and a tape dispenser to assemble the boxes with. She carefully padded and packed each box and filled a duffle with them to mail back to the Valley. The post office was close by, almost part of the airport, and in less than two hours she had the packages mailed home to the Golden Valley Store.

Josh was hungry again and wanted to find a hotel with a restaurant for the night, but Claire insisted they fly to Nome before it got dark: which would be around the end of August.

They compromised and had dinner at the Airport Café in the evening. Josh had crab legs and top sirloin and rice, while Claire had a salmon fillet and fries, soggy ones of course.

The flight to Nome took less than an hour but it was still pretty late so they stayed at the Sitnasuak Native Corporation's hotel for the night. Josh was surprised that there were several taxis in town. Their driver told Claire about local artists who were not drunks, at least most of the time. Claire knew of a few others so she had an idea on who to visit tomorrow. Josh had some ivory carvers to see, who he'd done business with on other buying trips to the area. So they agreed that tomorrow they'd separate and go on buying sprees alone. Claire knew as much about ivory as Josh, but ivory carvers were mainly men and the Eskimo culture says men dealt with men and women dealt with women. Except for the ivory and whale bone, Josh wondered, if Claire was a pilot, what would she need him for? He asked her that once. She said, "Keep your socks on Fly Boy."

The next day Josh visited a gun shop on the main drag in town and got a lead on a set of Purdy & Sons shotguns. He followed up by phoning and then visiting the niece of a retired and now deceased banker, who had taken the guns as security for a personal loan from a visiting hunter from England, who needed fifty bucks for a visit to a bordello one Saturday night after a successful ptarmigan hunt. He ended up shot dead in a poker game after doing the deed in the bordello, and drinking too much.

The card game wasn't the reason he got shot. During the game he bragged about his bedroom abilities, but said that the whore he saw was rather cold and had very bad breath: he

166

was promptly shot by the lady's husband, the card dealer, who thought his wife's breath was no worse than the average whore and that she was a very good lay!

Josh bought the guns for $200. Waiting for a taxi, he talked to a Native guy painting a boat in the lot next door. The painter said he had a cousin with a raw fresh Polar Bear skin that might be for sale. His cousin lived in Gambell on St. Lawrence Island, way out in the Bering Strait. Josh had planned to fly to Gambell to buy ivory, maybe tomorrow, weather permitting, and wondered if it might be best to go commercial with Bering Air, instead of flying the 170 mile trip in his single engine 206. However, if there really was a bear skin he'd have to take the 206: he knew Bering Air wouldn't fly a Polar Bear hide without an inch thick stack of paperwork and he didn't want the hassle.

Nome is not a small town, with almost 4,000 people. It's also the regional center of the eighteen outlying villages in the area. Gold mining is still big business, because of rising gold prices. Gold was now over $900 an ounce, and who knows what tomorrow will bring. Tourism is big too. The Native population has been in wonderment for the last century or so. Some Eskimos within 50 miles of Nome live as they did 200 years ago, yet other Eskimos drive taxis, own restaurants, run small construction companies, pilot aircraft, and do whatever any other person might do to make a living. The Sitnasuak Native Corporation's businesses are well managed and employ Natives and non Natives alike.

Sitnasuak and other Native Corporations were funded originally by the Native Claims Settlement Act, which paid Native Eskimos and Indians of the state nearly a Billion dollars to settle land disputes starting when the Russians originally claimed part of Alaska as their own. Many critics of the Act said the money would corrupt the innocent and do little to help the native people of the state. Were they ever wrong!

Claire was lamenting because less and less Native Arts

and Crafts are being made in Alaska and more "Crap" is being imported and sold as Alaskan Art. Jean knew that Josh had once bought Chinese Ivory as native, and she'd say, "What the hell does Josh know about ivory anyway?" Josh would argue, his wife signs the pay checks, so Jean should show a bit more respect: but he wouldn't say that too loud.

The morning of the following day was foggy. The marine layer wasn't lifting. Even Bering Air wasn't flying to Gambell today, so Josh and Claire were very definitely not going. They rented an old Ford, one of the only cars available, and took a ride down the coast to see the beach and one of the local tourist attractions: the "railroad to nowhere".

The train and track was a dream of a rail transportation promoter and a few rich and very easily influenced investors. The train was going to pull gold ore from several hard rock mines near Council, to a central processing mill in Nome. The very small narrow gauge train never made it as a business: some say it never even made the first trip, and for the last 100 years has been slowly sinking into the permafrost under the tundra.

They also saw a herd of Muskoxen that at first looked like old oil drums scattered around out on the tundra, until they started to move. Later in town they visited the "Board of Trade", which is reputed to have the longest bar of any saloon in the state. The bar is a thing of beauty. It's probably traded more gold for booze than any saloon north of Sacramento.

After returning the rental car they walked on the famous Nome Gold Beach. The place where anyone with a gold pan or even a pie plate could still find the precious golden metal so sought after since, forever. They avoided the gold seekers panning and digging sand for their small sluice boxes. Josh picked up a sea shell. Better than gold, maybe not, but pretty just the same. Josh was walking and talking with his gold: and he knew it.

# CHAPTER TWENTY-SEVEN

## — ST. LAWRENCE ISLAND —

WEDNESDAY MORNING was clear and calm with the forecast more of the same. Claire decided they needed adventure, by way of flying to Gambell on St Lawrence Island to find that bear skin. The plan was to fly to the Savoonga airport, in the middle of the island, find an ivory carver who Skip had recommended, see what he had to sell, and at least establish a working business relationship through the US mail.

Then they'd fly to Gambell on the northwest end of the island to see about the Polar Bear skin. Legitimate buyers had contacted Josh in the past, wanting a Polar Bear skin, raw and not tanned. There was also an Episcopal Priest who he'd talked to before, who wanted to help local artists, and had an idea about marketing ivory, for Josh to investigate.

The trip across the Bering Strait was uneventful, kind of boring. When landing at Savoonga airport they were met by a young Native with a taxi service. It consisted of a Honda Three Wheeler pulling a trailer with seats for two. Josh paid the driver $4 to pull the both of them to the home of Homer Rayle, the ivory carving artist who Skip had mentioned. Homer was home and happy to greet potential customers. He showed them three pieces of the highest quality carvings. Josh bought them on the spot for their asking price of $45 and shook hands on the deal.

Eskimos like to shake hands: the hand shake is not in their culture but they have adopted it and seem unable to shake hands without displaying a genuine smile, an honest genuine smile. Homer Rayle had three teeth: one on the top and two on the bottom. His smile was unbelievably sincere and he asked for the address of the Golden Valley Store. Claire gave Homer a business card and he fairly well beamed. He put it in a cigar box with two other cards: one from his Native Corporation, Sitnasuak, and the other was from Bering Air, the airline that services St Lawrence Island. Homer proudly showed Josh his share holder certificate in the Sitnasuak Corporation and a $545 dividend check, now six months old and still not cashed.

There was no place in Savoonga to cash a check. The bar owner from Nome does come once a month but charges a $50 cashing fee. Homer needed to go to Gambell or all the way to Nome to get his money, because a cashing fee was just plain stealing. Homer said he did not like to fly, and then Claire did a much unexpected thing, by offering to cash the check for him. Homer said it'd cost him $130 dollars to fly to Nome and he'd like to give Claire the $50 fee for cashing the check. Claire gave Homer the full face amount and said if Homer ever came to Fairbanks he should please come by the store and visit. Homer cried! He was as likely to visit Mars as he was Fairbanks but just the same he was overcome by the offer.

Homer's house was one room and a closet. The toilet was out back: the only indoor plumbing in Savoonga was at the airport and post office. Homer went into his closet and came out with a dozen more ivory carvings. These were not his carvings but were from other carvers who were now dead or had moved away. All had been friends of his. Before his wife died she had been collecting ivory and had not wanted to sell any. Homer really needed a three wheeler and was willing to sell the lot for $350. Before Josh had a chance to open the bargaining Claire said OK and gave Homer the money. So much for the Man on Man Native Culture.

They left Homer with another handshake and smile: thinking they'd walk back to the plane. The ivory was in her back pack. The kid who'd transported them down the hill to Homer's house was still there waiting. The trip would cost $5 this time because it was up hill. Claire jumped into bargaining and said $4 or no deal: the kid accepted with a smile and a hand shake and off they went to the airport.

When they got there Claire gave the kid $5. The kid had more teeth than Homer and equally as big a smile. Josh asked if by chance the kid knew of the fellow in Gambell with the

Polar Bear skin. The kid said a man by the name of Charlie Tom living right here in Savoonga had a Polar Bear skin and might want to sell it.

The bear had killed both of Charlie's dogs two days ago and had eaten most of them before Charlie killed it with his .22 caliber rifle. Josh really didn't believe a man could have killed a Polar Bear with a .22 but the kid insisted, Charlie shot it many times and the kill shot was right through the eye as the bear came toward him for another meal. The kid said that Charlie probably hadn't had a bath for several months and would've tasted like poop: might have!

So, for $5 more the kid took Josh and Claire to Charlie's house and sure as heck: a large bear skin was on a walrus skinning rack drying in the open air. Charlie knew the bear skin had some value and had started to celebrate his good fortune a little early. He was a mean little drunk with breath that could stop a stampede. Charlie wanted $350 for it but settled on $285. He wasn't friendly, did not shake hands, and wanted Josh and Claire gone as soon as they rolled up the skin. Claire insisted that Charlie sign both a bill of sale, and the skin, with a marking pen, in three separate places, before making payment. He agreed and seemed proud that he could sign his name. He either would not or could not read the bill of sale that described the raw Polar Bear Skin as a product of his Native Art.

The transportation costs were $6 this time because the skin was heavy: Claire thought it weighed a hundred pounds. She quickly paid the transport price before it went up again. On the way to the airport they took a small detour to look for high ground with a view of the west: out over the Bering Strait. They climbed the one small hill on the way to the airport and, standing on the top, could see Siberia. The view seemed never ending, truly spectacular, Josh was thinking.

Even though they were running a little short on money they flew north to the biggest town on the island, Gambell, to look for the other bear skin.

Josh landed the 206 at noon. Gambell has 600 residents and a Gun shop, an outboard motor/snow mobile sale and repair shop, and a large General Store and Café — all the modern conveniences of any small town in the middle of the Bering Strait, 130 miles from nowhere. The only indoor plumbing is at the post office, police station, and a few businesses. Indoor toilets, however, are popular because the town has a honey bucket hauler who comes around once a week to empty the sewage buckets. Most locals save their urine for acid tanning walrus and other skins. The solids go into honey buckets and are then stored in empty 55 gallon fuel barrels near the rocky ocean beaches. When the Bering Strait freezes up in the fall the barrels are rolled out on the ice and are gone as soon as the ice breaks up and floats away in the springtime. This solves the "empty barrel" problem which cost more to take back to Nome than anyone is willing to pay, and also solves the sewage disposal problems.

Claire was happy to visit the totally modern facilities indoors at the restaurant. Josh found a plethora of strangely tempting items on the menu, that he did not order. Lunch was served by a college student from Iowa who was traveling for the summer and had run out of money in Gambell. He said that he thought Gambell was probably the end of the earth. Josh said, "Maybe but, before you make that judgment, you might go to Savoonga for the real bitter end."

They had good hamburgers. The beef was from grass fed beef, slaughtered and delivered directly from Kodiak Island.

With lunch finished, Josh asked about directions to the address of the folks with the bear skin. The waiter knew exactly where the home was; he was staying at a long term Bed and Breakfast just down the street. The man who had the bear skin was a walrus hunter and fairly well to do: also well respected in the community. It was a half mile walk to the address.

When Claire and Josh arrived at the house, the skin was leaving in the hands of an already successful buyer, a gift shop

172

owner from Anchorage who Claire recognized. He and Claire spoke briefly about the sale and the buyer seemed to rub in the fact he'd gotten there first. He bragged that he'd paid only $2.8K for the skin which was about a third what it was really worth wholesale. He said, "Better luck next time, kid".

Claire asked if he might like to sell half or a third of it and he just laughed. He said he had willing buyers lined up and would do this deal 100% by himself. Then he said there was another skin available on the island and he intended to get that one too. Claire wondered loudly where it was, and he said he might tell her after he had the skin in hand. Claire asked if he'd let her have part of that deal, and he said no: not this time. She wished him luck and said she and Josh were on the Island mainly for Walrus ivory and other scrimshaw art. She didn't say that she already had the other skin. He said he had an oosik for her if she wanted. Claire turned and walked away. Her sense of humor and ability to spin a tale were among the things that Josh appreciated about her. There might also be a couple of 34 Bs.

Josh had one more stop. He visited the Episcopal Priest and worked out a detailed marketing plan for the local ivory artists on the Island, with the church as a 7% intermediary. Claire gave the Priest $100 to cover the cost of insuring the first shipment of ivory to the store.

By 4:00 they were ready to return. It took a little longer than usual because of an off shore breeze that slowed them a little. Claire insisted on rolling up the bear skin in the tent and wanted to take it with them to the hotel. She refused to leave $20,000 worth of ivory and skins in the plane on the un-guarded ramp for the night. Josh was opposed, but when Claire insisted, he offered to just fly back to Bettles and they could spend the night with Molly and Kevin Ferguson. Josh could probably lock up the plane in Kevin's hanger for the night and they would be home from their weeklong trip in just four days. Josh fueled the plane, and they were off at 6:30 for a three hour trip to Bettles. Josh put the ball to the wall and went to 11,000 ft. The three hour trip took 2:22 minutes. Claire was impressed that at altitude and lightly loaded the Cessna 206 is not at all slow.

On short final going into Bettles, Josh was surprised to see a familiar Super Cub running up on the ramp. Kevin was happy to see Josh and Claire and welcomed them for the night. Molly had cooked a moose roast with potatoes but they had already eaten. While Claire and Josh ate, Kevin and Molly had a second desert and coffee. With the 206 locked in the hanger, life seemed to be going well. When asked about the Super Cub, Kevin said there'd been lots of traffic going up and down the Coleville River, no more than usual but many folks looked like they belonged in Chicago, not Bettles. Patten leather shoes and attaché cases do not go well at a bush airport.

Josh told Kevin about the cut and acid corroded control cables on the 185 and how picking up the 206 in a trade. He did not tell Kevin about the diamond scam, or "the diamond situation", depending on how you looked at it. That was no one's business except Carter's, and Josh thought it a violation of trust if he spread around the story. Kevin asked, who cut the cables, and Josh said the FBI wouldn't even look into it because all the cables were removed from the plane before anyone had a chance to investigate. But just the same he thought he knew who it was and there would be paybacks the next time they met. The FBI probably thought it was a cover up for sloppy maintenance and unless the NTSB pushed, nothing further would happen. Josh also mentioned to Kevin about the little dab of white paint he'd put on each and every inspection plate on the 206. He could tell at a glance during his walk around whether or not any of the plates had been removed: it would not happen again.

# CHAPTER TWENTY-EIGHT

## — PROBLEMS BACK AT THE STORE —

MOLLY INVITED Claire to pick Blue Berries the next morning and Josh and Kevin went fishing for Grayling. After catching a dozen they cleaned them and enjoyed the added treat to the trip. Still, Josh wanted to get home but Claire was so relaxed they spent most of the day just visiting their friends. About 4:00 they decided to fly back and dine at the Ivory Exchange to celebrate the success of their craft and skin buying trip. Josh was equally proud of the Purdy and Sons shotguns he bought. They were valuable. He planned to keep one and sell the other.

The flight from Bettles took an hour ten and twelve gallons of fuel. They flew to Fairbanks International to fuel up first. Josh added a quart of oil and washed the windshield before the short flight to the Goldstream Valley.

When they landed behind the store and pulled up behind the loading dock, Claire wondered about Angel. She almost always greeted the plane and it was the only time Claire ever heard her bark. Josh wheeled in so the cargo door was close to the loading dock, pulled out the mixture control, and shut down the engine. The master switch off he set his parking brake and chocked the front tire to secure the plane for the night.

Josh felt pretty cocky about the trip. The polar bear hide was an unexpected find and he was sure it'd pay all the bills for the trip and then some.

They entered thru the back door. Carter and Jean were standing together, looking out toward the front of the store.

Josh: "Carter, nice to see you: what're you doing here?"

Carter: "I came out for dinner next door and stopped to say Hi. Jean said you were out buying ivory"

Jean turned and said, "Welcome back, JJ, how'd the trip go? How's my favorite old CJ doing?"

Claire felt for her 38 in her shoulder holster. Jean would never ever refer to them like that unless there was trouble.

Claire: "We did just fine. Oops, I forgot something in the plane, just a minute, I'll be right back in."

Josh: "Jean, what happened, you've got a bloody nose?"

Claire quickly went back out toward the plane, as Jim Littlejohn showed himself.

Littlejohn: "Good afternoon, Josh, my friends and I have come for a visit. We might've called first, but we're such good friends, I felt it unnecessary. My big buddy Bob, Mike Thompson, his Pit Bull, and myself are here to pick up the diamonds. My investors want them. Either I get them or I will tear this place up and you with it. I'll also like to introduce Angel to 'Sampson the Bull'. Too bad she's at the Vets."

Littlejohn had what looked like a Glock pistol and Bob, the guy who'd been with David, an Ithaca pump shotgun.

Jean: "They showed up 10 minutes ago, Casey's in school, and Angel's at the Vets on Farmer's Loop getting her teeth cleaned."

Josh knew there was no truth there. Casey was off for the summer to write her thesis and should've been at the store clerking this afternoon. Angel might be anywhere but the Vets.

Littlejohn: "Shut the hell up, Jean. Josh, just where are my diamonds? You've 30 seconds to hand over my diamonds, or forever wish you had."

Josh: "I don't have any diamonds. I'm just a Valley store keeper. I don't sell diamonds. I sell groceries, gas, whiskey, and a little ivory, but not diamonds."

Mike Thompson: "Josh, I've a great deal of cash invested here, where are the diamonds?"

Josh: "Mike, I thought you were FBI? What're you doing looking for diamonds, I have no diamonds."

Mike: "Cut the crap, Josh. I'm a PI who also happens to be an investor in the Coleville Mining and Exploration Co."

Carter: "There are no diamonds, there never were any diamonds. We were looking for gold and platinum at that site on the Coleville. We found a little gold. We think there's some copper too, but not enough to mine profitably. There are no diamonds in Alaska Everybody knows that!"

Littlejohn: "Mike, there were diamonds. Pete told me there were Diamonds, he saw them!"

Carter: "What is this crap? Pete's a lying little prick! Did you ever see diamonds?"

Littlejohn: "Pete said there were diamonds, so there are."

Bob, shotgun in hand, stepped forward toward Josh. Angel came bounding thru the front entrance, jumped high, and hit him with her full weight, at the center of his back. He tumbled forward. Josh grabbed the Ithaca to avoid being hit by it. Bob slammed down hard across the potato chip display.

Jean: "You're going to pay for those chips, they don't grow on trees, you know."

Bob: "Screw you, Jean!"

Jean: "Don't you wish."

Littlejohn was totally pissed off, but not sure of anything anymore. He pointed his Glock, ready to take a shot at Josh when Jean nailed him with an accurate kick to his manly parts. She had on high heeled, pointy-toed cowboy boots, to give her 5'3" height a boost, to comfortably work the counter and run the register. The boots also made her the proper height to nail Jim Littlejohn right where it most counted. He fired his Glock twice. Josh was already moving and Jean's kick deflected Jim's aim. One bullet hit the floor and the other the Coke cooler door, splattering safety glass across the floor. Buckled over, Jim wanted to shoot again, when Claire came through the front entrance. Littlejohn turned toward her. She shot him in the right shoulder with her .38. His Glock flew out of his hand, into the Liquor Department, and landed on the floor, where it skidded to a stop in front of the display of the Marlboro man on horseback.

It seemed pretty much over, when Mike Thompson pulled a revolver from a well fitting shoulder holster. He aimed at Claire. Josh smashed in his face with the butt end of the

177

Ithaca shotgun, that Bob had almost handed him as he fell. Mike staggered backwards, caught his balance, and would have shot Claire, if Josh hadn't broken his knee with an oddly placed kick, not meant for his knee. Then Josh again struck fast with the Ithaca and smashed Mike's head with the gun barrel. Angel grabbed Mike's arm and backed away hard, keeping him stretched out prone. Josh grabbed away the revolver. He now had a gun in each hand, with neither in shooting position. Bob got up off the floor and jumped head first, diving over the counter separate the groceries from the liquors, and came up with Littlejohn's Glock. Jean climbed onto the counter near the cash register, reached for the Mini 14, hidden behind the cigarette display, and jacked a shell into the chamber. She would've shot Bob but couldn't: she was too high to see thru the door way. Bob backed out of the store and down the front steps quickly, threatening murder to anyone who followed.

But then his lights went out. He'd been decked by a two piece McDermott Knight M-29AD Series Pool Cue, which was now in three pieces. Tommy, gentle quiet Tommy, had just run another table.

Claire: "I always said Tommy's better with a cue than anyone I ever met. We should get him a first place trophy for 'Best bank shot', or something like that: what do you think?"

Josh: "The safety was on, or I would've shot the bastard. It's a left-handed safety. Who the hell comes to a gun fight with the safety on? What a weird jerk!"

Then the pit bull attacked Angel, who was totally caught off guard, as she was dealing with Mike Thompson. Instantly a hell of a fight ensued: the dogs rolled around on the floor, around and over Mike. He could barely see through the blood from his smashed nose and forehead, and tried to get clear, but couldn't because his knee didn't work. He kept trying to get up, and then falling into the middle of a dog fight.

The pit bull was  shorter than Angel but much stronger. Don from the Exchange had heard the gun shots and ran over to see what was happening. Their pup Spider was with him and the little guy ran right into the middle of the fight, trying to help Angel, but Spider was quickly torn, grabbed full jaw, bitten badly, and thrown all the way across the store by the pit bull. Spider was down and fully out just that quick, bloody, and seemly not breathing.

Angel got the pit bull by the throat and ripped and shook him, but the bull was not giving up.

Josh finally shifted the shotgun safety to off but couldn't get a clean shot at the pit bull, without the chance of hitting Angel. Claire stepped in close and blasted the pit bull right in the ear with her .38.

Littlejohn was hit but trying to stand, Bob was out for the count. Mike's face was bloodied. He'd a broken knee, could only see out of one eye, and his arms and hands were torn up: one of the dogs had bit his hand thru and thru. It was bleeding badly. Still, he was in better shape than the other two, of what was left of the Fargo Group, or as Jean later called them: "The Fargoett's."

Casey came down the stairs wearing only a towel, and toting one of Claire's hand guns. She'd been in the apartment shower when she heard the shots. She pointed the revolver straight out. Her towel hooked the potato chip display and dropped.

Josh: "Not bad for a PhD candidate. What do you think Claire? Kind of reminds me of when we first met, you know, before gravity."

Claire: "I guess this means Superman doesn't really have x-ray vision."

Casey wrapped her towel back in place. "I want Hazard and Modeling Pay, when you can get around to it."

From the counter, Jean jumped to the floor with the Mini 14. She told Mike, "Get the hell away from our wood stove. Blood is corrosive to antiques. Crawl off."

Two patrol cars with sirens blaring skidded to a stop and

almost hit Bob, sitting in the parking lot shaking his head and trying to recover his senses. The Troopers took control and wanted to know exactly what had been going on. Carter assumed the job of spokesman for the store and tried to put the events in sequence. He hadn't done much to improve things but at least didn't get in the way. He claimed to be a friend and customer and was, according to the Troopers, "an uninvolved third party" who they totally believed, probably because he was dressed so well. He looked great!

According to Carter, "Jim Littlejohn and his goons parked their car in the Exchange parking lot and went to the store with mayhem on their minds, and that pit bull, the dead one over there. The big guy Bob bragged that 'the Pitt Bull was going to tear up the store's guard dog, Angel, and then get that bitch' Claire, and that's a quote! When Jean, the lady with the bloody nose, saw them coming, she stood in the doorway to stop them. Jim Littlejohn pushed past her looking, for Claire and Josh, and she pushed back. Littlejohn took a swing at Jean and knocked her down."

Jean: "That's also why he's not walking too well."

She turned to Littlejohn. "What a man you are, you can beat up a girl, you pathetic wimp!"

Carter continued to describe the fight accurately: he went on until the Troopers were quite well informed, but not totally.

When the three bad guys were handcuffed, Claire took Angel and what was left of Spider to the vet on Farmer's Loop Rd. Tommy said Spider could be an organ donor. "Are there organ donors for dogs?" he asked. Claire said she'd call with news as soon as she could.

The Troopers took Littlejohn's crew away and the dead pit bull as well, to finish photographing him.

Carter said, "The Troopers know about these guys selling drugs, and distributing Oxy and Heroin, the really bad stuff."

Jean went with the Troopers to file the complaints. The loggers across the street had called the Troopers who came within minutes. They must have been close.

Claire called a little later to say, "The vet said Angel and Spider, though badly beat up, had no broken bones and would survive just fine." Spider had been in shock and breathing very slowly. The vet also said that puppies have soft bones that bend instead of break, so Spider was unbroken. He is just one big bruise with enough stitches to make a formal gown, but Angel was in worse shape and would take longer to heal. A few of her ribs were cracked, her missing toe nails would grow back, but she'd have some trouble with her left hip for a while. She also had stitches in her lips and nose, and the vet sewed up most of her left ear. Angel had a deep bite on her back too. Just the same she was coming home. The vet had given her a shot for pain and some real good ear rubs, on her right ear.

Claire carried her to the van, then went back for Spider. She put Spider next to Angel and Angel licked Spider's nose. Claire drove slowly. When she arrived at the store, the front door was open. The Liquor display lights were on in the front windows. Claire looked at her watch: 8:20, still forty minutes till closing. Casey was dressed and busy restocking the beer cooler. The door on the Coke cooler was patched with plywood. Josh had already mopped up the blood and bleached the floor in front of the potato chip display, where the Pitt bull had died. Skip was running the cash register just like he owned the place, and he had funny smile on his face that reminded Claire of their younger days. A funny thing about Skip: he somehow always shows up at the right time.

Claire carried Angel, all 75 pounds of her, to the old wood stove that was now cold. She went back and got Spider to deliver him into the Ivory Exchange by the back door.

Carter called and said he and Jean would be back to the store after Jean got her nose re-set in the emergency room at the Hospital, close to the Trooper's Post on Peger Rd.

Josh decided they'd stay open late, to commemorate their successful buying trip to the west coast, and to celebrate the ass-kicking of Littlejohn and crew.

Carter and Jean arrived a half hour later. The sun had set in the North West, but twilight was such that lights were unnecessary, unless you wanted to read a newspaper or something. Jean's nose was fully bandaged. When Don saw her, he thought she still looked pretty, for a girl.

Carter wasn't sure exactly what to do or say. He was truly the root cause of all of this, but was still liked. Josh and Claire could have stopped supplying liquor to the camp at any time, but they didn't. Neither did they blame Carter for any of the injury and grief. They fully blamed the Cartel from Fargo and wondered if they'd ever hear from the that group again.

As the quiet of the night crept into the Valley, displacing the hurly-burly of their day, the friends of yesterday realized they had become a very eclectic but strangely solid family.

It turned out, Jean had called Skip earlier, before having her nose set in the emergency room, to ask if he had a good attorney. Skip wanted to know what was wrong. When Jean told him, Skip immediately drove out to the Valley to support his friends. That's how he got the word. It wasn't telepathy as Claire had wondered.

Don was really disturbed by what had happened, especially to Spider, and asked Skip about an NRA course on firearm safety. Neither Don or Tommy had ever owned a gun but they wanted one now.

Josh wondered out loud what might've happened if Jean hadn't called him JJ, when he and Claire arrived. Casey hadn't been involved, but the conflict concerned and still frightened her. She wondered if it was alright to sleep on the couch in the apartment, to not be alone.

Skip asked about the polar bear skin Josh brought in and showed off. Both men figured it might be worth $12,000 to the right buyer. Angel limped to each person present for a rub. Even hurting, she wondered if someone might have a jerky strip for her somewhere.

# Chapter Twenty-Nine

## — *The Littlejohn Problem* —

CLAIRE AND CASEY opened the store at 9:00 am just like any other Friday morning. Josh carried Angel down the stairs: she was moving very slowly but still doing her patrol work, by walking around the store every hour. She was the center of attention suddenly and she really liked that. So many ear rubs and so much beef jerky were unexpected but very nice.

Josh was on the phone most of the morning. He'd an appointment to see a Detective in the afternoon. Jean had already given her view of the attack. She was pressing Assault and Battery charges with the Assistant District Attorney. Friday was a tough day to get anything done at the Troopers Post on Peger Road but Burt Curwen, Trooper Detective, planned to keep Jim Littlejohn in the lockup for the weekend, by slowing down the booking process, so he could sort out the charges.

Casey thought that was a great idea but wondered what else was going on. Josh guessed that Casey and Claire might already be working on the movie script.

The attorney for the jailed men tried to get a judge to issue a writ for the release of the pair. Bail was not yet set and the charges were not felonious yet. The ADA was being rather cautious. Casey, with her youthful idealism, was furious. She wanted to show the lawyer what felonious was all about.

Don was more pragmatic. He just wanted to get a Carry Concealed Permit. To his surprise, Alaska did not have such a permit. At the time no law said you could and no law said you could not carry a concealed firearm.

Don drove into Fairbanks, parked his car next to Samson's Hardware, and walked around the corner and down the street a ways. He descended a flight of stairs and into "Guns Down Under", with intentions of getting an education on fire-arms. Then and there he bought a 9 mm Glock 19, ammunition, a shoulder holster, and signed up for a NRA class.

The District Attorney finally agreed to charge the villains with First Degree Assault and add Battery in the second degree for Jim Littlejohn.. Felonious Assault demands a high bail but the attorney produced the $50,000 cash bond in less than 20 minutes. It took the clerk the better part of ten minutes to count the hundred dollar bills. So much for a weekend in jail.

Back in Goldstream, Don set a up very short target range on the far side of the restaurant, and he and Casey shot a few paper bad guys. He was OK direction wise but elevation control was rather poor. Casey told him to shoot left handed. He was amazingly better then, at holding the weapon steady as he squeezed the trigger. The police had taken all but two of the guns. They somehow thought the Ithaca shotgun was Claire's. After cleaning it up and removing the blood, Josh realized the Ithaca was a 5E Grade skeet gun: a real collector's item. Since he was a collector it only made sense to keep it. The police also missed accounting for Mike Thompson's revolver that Josh had taken from him. Josh gave it to Tommy, so he and Don could take NRA gun safety class together. Tommy decided togetherness was good. Josh thought, if Tommy's pool cue skills transferred to the pistol, Tommy would be a fine shot. That made no sense, so it must be true.

The weekend was quiet, Claire cataloged and priced the ivory from the Nome trip and bought an extra display case for the added inventory. Having spent so much money, Josh and Claire had to go back to being store keepers. Tommy paid a carpenter to put a pet door in back of his restaurant. Angel used it as much as Spider. They were buddies!

Josh found a potential buyer for the bear skin and spent the best part of Sunday building a stretching and drying frame. Josh was sure now that the skin would bring $14,000, since legally it was Native Art work, signed in three places, harvested and sold by a Native Artist. Josh had cleared it with Alaska Fish and Game but he was still a bit worried, because the Feds were involved: polar bears were on the endangered species listings.

Skip told Josh that he and Martha were going to the east coast to visit Martha's parents in rural Vermont. It looked to Claire as though Skip would tie the knot again, but Josh was not too sure. He saw that Skip was sincere but thought Martha wanted her freedom, and figured Skip was nice for awhile but not forever.

Meanwhile, the Goldstream Valley was quiet and tranquil and only disturbed by a few subtle zephyrs flowing down the verdant Aspen covered hillsides. Lazy breezes rattled the Aspen and Birch to imitate the sounds of a million butterflies. The rivers ran slowly but steadily. Every life form relaxed just a little. In the Valley, summer is as gentle as the winter is rogue.

After a few weeks, some Goldstream residents started to prepare for winter. They spent the long days cutting and splitting the winter's supply of wood. Some hauled and banked coal, from the bunkers near the rail yard in town to their own storage sheds. In the dead of winter, the coal seemed much farther from the door and the stove.

As Josh predicted, five weeks after Skip left, he came back to Fairbanks alone. Martha decided to stay in Vermont and care for her parents. Skip knew it was more than likely he would not see Martha again. She had said, Skip was just a little too much outlaw for her, and at his age he couldn't change. Skip might change for the right woman, but Martha was not the one.

## CHAPTER THIRTY

### — ONE YEAR LATER —

THREE SEASONS came and went. Goldstream valley residents survived yet another winter. Fairbanks was still booming, just not quite as much as it had during the height of the pipe line construction.

Jim Littlejohn and the two other men were fined heavily for assault and battery and placed on probation for one year's time. As part of their probation, they were to have no contact with the Golden Valley Store or any store employees. Two of the men moved out of state, and Jim Littlejohn and his son managed the mining operation on the north slope near the town of Umiat on the Coleville River. They seldom came to Fairbanks and seemed to cause no problems.

Skip came by the store in the late afternoon and said he found out some really interesting news about the Fargo Cartel, from a friend of his in Detroit, dying of cancer. The news was that the Fargo Cartel had been taken over by a group out of Reno Nevada and there'd be no further diamond mining. Mike, the guy with the unfortunate knee, had objected to the take-over and quietly left the cartel. Jim Littlejohn was also on someone's shit list in Reno and had been told to get a new act.

Skip said the story was now that the strip mine on the Coleville is a gold mine. Period: a gold mine. The hunt for any kind of diamonds was finished and not even being mentioned. Also, the Reno group didn't deal drugs and Littlejohn better mind his new bosses: no more drug sales, or else. Skip asked, "How long do you think he can leave easy drug money alone?"

In any case, Josh, Carter, Skip, and Pete were the only ones who ever saw the stones and maybe they were lucky, nobody important ever believed them. No one has seen Pete in a year's time either, but he had said he was going to Hawaii for a month, before he vanished completely.

Claire thought there might have been other clear crystals

that Carter was just calling diamonds, maybe Cubic Zirconium or the like. Since Carter was never concerned that Angel had run away with the satchel, she figured there was little value there: the stones were just part of the scam, which made sense but Angel's disappearance with the stones was still a mystery to Claire.

Then again, Angel would beg for a pancake at breakfast, take it away, and hide it so it was never seen again. Angel was super smart but not very logical, at least in people logic. Josh fully expected her to show up with the satchel any day but Claire is not convinced. Maybe Angel just liked the smell and taste of the leather satchel and could care less as to its contents, whatever it might be.

Skip had a sense of the larger picture though: "The story is, the folks who put up the money to buy the leases are letting Jim Littlejohn manage the entire strip mining operation, and he's planning to lease equipment, to keep the capitol investment down, till the sluicing operation starts after the spring breakup, which sounds like a 6th grade business development idea, good for a lemonade stand. Hell, getting heavy equipment to the site is a major logistical problem. You don't fly in a D6 Cat or a big loader in a Cessna. You need a real cargo plane, a C130 Hercules transport, and a hell of a lot more runway than is there now. You need mechanics to assemble the heavy pieces. Littlejohn might know how to transport illegal drugs, but mining's a little more difficult. Littlejohn is in way over his tiny head. He is still on supervised probation from the District Court too. He's no problem but his own, from now on, I think."

Josh almost felt sorry for the guy, almost. He found it hard to believe that there were gem quality diamonds to be found on the Coleville in the first place, and now the same fools were looking for gold in the exact same place: made no sense at all. "You could still haul the small stuff for them, Josh."

Josh: "It'd depend on the profit margin and whether or not I've had a lobotomy."

Skip: "Even if there is gold, how would a hood from Fargo, North Dakota find it?"

Josh: "If they hired a guy like Earl Pilgrim to oversee the project. You think that's why they talked to him?"

Skip: "My guess is they'll find a young Mining Engineer to at least consult with. There are a couple working up in the Livengood District right now, on closed circuit hydraulic gold projects. John Berglund is doing contract work there, but he's expensive and no dummy. He'd know that there's no gold and wouldn't take the job."

Carter was still a security consultant for Alyeska and still worked for the Seven Sisters. He might need charter flying for the oil company Big Wigs, but Josh would still recommend Grizzly Air to him, just down the strip a 100 yards: Josh just plain did not want to fly people: he liked cargo.

In the fall Casey stopped working full time, so as to finish Graduate School. She studied upper atmosphere chemistry and proved some of her assumptions and disproved others, regarding the physics of refrigerant gasses as they migrated into the Troposphere.

A new group had formed at the Geophysical Institute involved with remote sensing of the earth's surface with photos, spectrum analysis, Synthetic Aperture Radar returns, and other data obtained from low earth orbiting satellites. This group also recorded conditions below satellite orbits, those that could be sampled by aircraft. The data structured the ideas in her thesis.

Claire helped Casey, but she was also helping herself, to understand and apply Remote Sensing to Geology investigations, beyond a chipping hammer and Shanks Mare.

Jean Managed the store during the summer like she owned it, and mostly treated Josh and Claire like hired help. Two of Casey's undergraduate college friends worked there full time now as Casey began interning at the Mapco North Pole Refinery. She had a work ethic second only to Jean.

Josh and Claire split the store's profits with Jean, giving

one third of the profit to the store, one third to themselves, and one third to Jean, in addition to their hourly pay and benefits. Jean wanted to install a time clock but Josh put his foot down and when it arrived he sent it straight back to the distributor: he neglected to mention this to Jean for a few weeks, until he got enough nerve to admit the deed.

It'd been more than a year since Josh bought the 206 and he'd been hauling food and other critical supplies to many of the smaller mining operations. Goldstream Aviation Services turned a steady profit. With the price of gold going up again, as rapidly as it was, Fairbanks was booming with startups.

Business leaders in Fairbanks grew ever more hopeful. Hope however seldom equals reality and those who could see past tomorrow scaled back. Gold wouldn't replace oil. The days of Alyeska Purchasing Managers going to local Chevy and Ford dealers and buying every 4X4 pickup in stock were over.

Gambling, drug, and prostitution operators, were still in high gear. There's a story about two truckers who bought a new Fright Liner tractor for over $125,000 and spent the summer pulling loads to Deadhorse, making around $5,000 per load. They'd financed most of the cost of the truck and were within $4,500 of having it paid for. On their way back on the haul road, passing through Fox, they flipped a coin to see if they'd pay off the note or spend a few days at Ruthie's on 23rd. Ruthie's won the flip and the truckers, while still having a small note on their truck, smiled all the way to Deadhorse on the next haul north.

Skip's restaurant, "The Gold Bar and Lounge" was less than 100 yards, as the Crow flies; from the infamous 2 Street (Second Avenue) row of bars, but it's a mile away in clientele. Skip kept a first class customer base and if you were unshaven, or needed a bath, were loud, or vulgar, you'd get no service at the "Gold Bar". And if you insisted, as drunks tend to do, you would be shown the door: either forwards or backwards.

Claire started a mineral exploration consulting business

using her geology skills along with new source of Geotechnical data that she and Casey had discovered. Claire had found that satellite photos, radar data, and other information, available only from satellite observations, could be obtained from the Geophysical Institute at the U of A, almost free of charge.

In her new business she billed her services at $100 an hour, plus expenses, or a little more than the $13.50 she made as a clerk at the Golden Valley Store. When she did travel Claire hired Goldstream Aviation Services to do her charters. She was about the only paying passenger that the crabby bush pilot would allow in his plane: a Cessna 206.

Claire and Josh bought a small house with a nice hanger just down the airstrip 200 yards from the store: it was a smaller home but had a guest bedroom and an office for her business. Josh got a heated office in the hanger.

Angel now had two places to take care of. She also looked after Spider at the Exchange.

Jean moved into the apartment above the store, rent free of course because she was the Manager. She found a washing machine mechanic to replace Josh and he was quite pleased to not deal with missing socks any longer.

Then, strangely, Skip started to show up at the store, for no apparent reason, except to spend time with Jean, and Jean started to like it. To say the opposites attract is poetic but not often true. Jean was as opposite to Skip as vinegar is to honey. Skip did, however, respect the ladies around him and tone his language down when Claire or Jean were present: mostly.

Skip was in his mid 50s, not really young, but he was as tough as nails. He didn't back down from anything or anybody, and he very decisively marched to his own music. Jean saw him drag two bikers, by the collars of their leather jackets, out of the Ivory Exchange and into the parking lot. Tommy had beaten one of them out of a few hundred dollars playing pool and the biker said he didn't know Fairies could shoot pool that well. Skip was at the bar having a beer at the time. The bikers claimed Tommy had cheated and planned to punch Tommy's "little pink lights out". Skip was having none of that: he finished his beer and then took exception to the biker's attitude with extreme prejudice. Skip thought, since he once owned the Exchange, he had a right to protect it, and his friends, and he did just that. Jean seemed to respect Skip's honesty: what she saw was what she got: every single time.

In the fall after the diamond issue was but a memory, one of the supposed FBI agents, Noel Simpson, the Jack Webb look-alike, came by the store to ask about the new gold mining operation going on up on the North Slope near the Coleville. He talked to Jean, then Claire and he was fairly hostile. They both did the Sergeant Schultz imitation and said they knew nothing. Noel Simpson then found Josh at the Exchange bar and started asking questions about Carter and what exactly the relationship between the store and Carter's security group was.

Josh said there was no relationship, that he'd hauled some booze for Carter and some business group, he forgot the name, but that the delivery business was no longer going on. When Josh questioned Noel about the FBI thing, Noel got nasty, so Josh told him to get lost. Noel asked Josh to step outside to the parking lot for a "tilt".

Josh: "What is this, the 1960s? A tilt? Are you a high school mascot? Take your phony badge and your phony smile and shove them where the sun doesn't shine!"

Noel put his hands on Josh and turned him around and off his bar stool. Noel assumed a classic karate stance and —

# Chapter Thirty-One
## — BYE BYE NOEL —

NOEL HIT THE FLOOR so hard the folks at the pool tables in the lounge heard it.. He was a long time getting up and then just walked, kind of sideways, out the front door: Noel no longer had his 9mm Glock. Josh took it, stuffed it into his belt and asked the bar tender for a second beer.

Skip had been playing pool with Tommy and almost won a game, but after losing $6 in six games, he wandered out to the bar to talk to Josh for a while.

Close to 8:00 Josh decided to walk down the road to see the "Love of his life" in living color: private joke. It was 8:01, while passing a phone pole, when his lights went out.

He woke up on the sofa in his front room, it was 9:20. He thought he heard his plane landing and saw the landing lights on a 206 go by the front room window. Claire was in the kitchen fixing dinner and Angel was next to him, sitting there just looking at him: not doing anything but looking at him. His head hurt and he had a serious lump on the right side of his neck and head, and a cut lip.

"What the hell happened? Man, this hurts!"

Claire: "I think you fell down. How much did you drink?"

Josh: "Just a couple of beers"

Claire: "Well, Skip found you on the ground and carried you here. Welcome home, Superman."

Josh: "Did I hear the plane just land?"

Claire: "No, Skip just taxied it down from the store. It'll be safer in the hanger: it looks like snow a little later tonight, and we won't have to brush the snow off in the morning."

The side door opened and Skip walked in, nodded to Claire, and pulled a beer out of the refrigerator.

Skip: "Welcome back to the real world, fly boy."

Josh: "Only Claire calls me fly boy, OK Ivory!"

Skip: "OK, truce? You were wobbly I decided to see if you

got home and found you on the ground near the telephone pole. You Ok? You had entirely too much to drink."

Josh: "I did not, really Claire, I did not. I was coming home to invite you to dinner at the Exchange. I must've slipped or whatever. Want to have dinner there?"

Claire: "Let's have dinner here, Superman. The walk might be too much for you."

Skip: "I'm gone, I've a date with a clerk, named Jean, do you know her?"

Josh saw Skip's right hand, gloved, blood seeping through the leather seams over his knuckles. Josh asked about this, and Skip said, "I scraped my hand while helping you to your feet."

Skip left, but Josh still felt a little dizzy. He checked for the Glock that he took from Noel in the bar, sure he'd put it in back under his belt. The Glock was gone. He asked Claire if she had it. Claire said she knew nothing about it.

After a while, when he felt better, Josh took a flash light and walked back toward the Exchange, to the phone pole where he was told he fell. There was nothing there. He decided to check the 206 and make sure Skip had turned the master switch off. He entered the hanger from the side door. The master was in fact off, and Josh found the missing Glock in the pilot seat side pocket.

# CHAPTER THIRTY-TWO

## — CARTER STOPS BY —

IN THE FALL OF THE YEAR, early September, when the Aspen and Birch in the Goldstream Valley turned truly golden, Carter Thomas stopped by the store to talk to Josh, who'd gone into Fairbanks to the post office and the Northward Hub to pick up supplies for a four man gold mining operation in Kantishna.

Carter said, "I'll wait at the Ivory Exchange and keep my eye out for his van."

Jean: "If he stops in here first I'll tell him and, oops, there he goes now, heading straight to the hanger."

Carter: "Thanks Jean, I'll catch him there."

Angel came in from her guard post under the front porch swing and never got a chance to say Hi or get an ear rub. She was 100% healthy now and back on guard duty full time. Angel followed Carter's car down the road a ways, then took a short-cut to the hanger. She stood next to Josh, when Carter walked through the back door, past the large stock of Ballantines Beer for the miners. "Hi Josh, how's it going?"

"Just fine, Carter. To what do I owe this visit? How's the security business treating you?"

Carter said his security business was still secure, and smiled. He needed a pilot to fly the length of the pipeline on a weekly basis, to photograph the route. He was under contract to Alyeska and no longer working directly for the Seven Sisters.

The deal was that the EPA was demanding the photos to ensure the safety of the pipeline, and so they could tell people they're really in command of anything and everything. Alyeska was all to happy to provide whatever the EPA wanted.

"You'd fly North and photograph the line one week and fly South to photograph the line the next week. It'll be easy and pay fairly well. Alyeska will stand the cost of modifying the plane and supply and pay for installing a motorized 35mm camera and a controller system. It's a yearlong contract at first and most likely be renewed year after year if the surveillance, is done properly, to the standards and satisfaction of the EPA and Alyeska's primary insurance carriers.

Carter continued, "Most people don't understand that operating a public conveyance, and the pipeline is a public conveyance, is a cost plus operation. At 7%, if you want to earn $7 you have to spend $100. If you want to earn $700, you find a way to spend $10,000. Money spent satisfying EPA requirements is simply more profit for the pipeline operators, so Alyeska welcomes added demands by the EPA. Want the job?"

Josh: "I think not, but I know someone who might like to think about it. Matt Smith; he has my old 185 and has been flying for Bud Hastings. He may have had it with Assistant Guide duties: lots of work and not much pay or glory. He's the guy to contact. I recommend him: honest, hard working, smart, and a pretty good pilot now. He has a dumpy looking hanger, but don't judge him by that, at International on the west side by the old C46s. It's convenient to pick up clients there and a good place to store sundry camping gear and other necessities. The rent's quite a bit cheaper than on the East Side ramp. If he's kept Bud happy, I'm sure he can make you happy also."

Carter agreed and changed the subject to the strip mining efforts on the Coleville River. He'd heard, that Jim Littlejohn was running a pretty tight operation and finding some fairly large gold nuggets, jewelry grade gold.

Josh: "That's not possible. There's no gold there. None!"

Carter: "Friends have seen and purchased fairly large nuggets from them. I'm sure of it."

Josh: "I suggest you don't invest in a Coleville River mine."

Carter: "His Reno investors aren't nervous anymore."

Josh: " I heard the site's run by drug dealers, not miners."

Carter: "Just the same the boys who put up the money seem to be getting results."

Josh: "There's no gold there. Claire's a Geologist and knows: there is no gold on the Coleville: trust me."

Carter: "Gold or not, his investors are happy: Strangely I did hear that he's back in drug distribution. I wonder how that will settle out."

Josh did a flash back to when Skip said the Reno folks told Littlejohn to stay out of the drug business.

Carter: "Anyway, if and when anyone comes asking, just plead ignorance: you were and you still are. One of the Cartel hoods, masquerading as a FBI Special Agent, disappeared a year back. I wonder if maybe Littlejohn did him in, no one knows."

Carter rubbed Angel's ear and left. She thought he was neat! Jean called from the store: Claire was looking for Josh with some news. Meanwhile, would he please put the chicken in the oven at 250.

Josh found the chicken in the fridge in a casserole dish. He squeezed out a serious dollop of barbecue sauce on top and put it in the oven as asked. He also found a package of Tater Tots in the freezer. Tater Tots and roast chicken. Could be worse. Angel thought maybe not.

Claire had taken on a consulting job for one of Alyeska's many civil engineering contractors, finding a good route for a road construction project from the old Taps Road to some low yield oil fields a little west of the Coleville River, near the foothills of the Brooks Range. For weeks she searched through satellite photos and radar images looking for solid ground with a minimum of permafrost, for a low maintenance and stable roadway. It had to be near or on gravel deposits of an ancient river bed, even if it went a little out of the way from the old Taps road, to be continuous. She found it. She also found unexpected formations in the land suggesting very old volcanic activity, taking place long before tectonic plate movements pushed up the Brooks Range, tens of millions of years ago, by using computer analysis of the Synthetic Aperture Radar results from the Remote Sensing lab at the Geophysical Institute. She was now sure of her interpretations.

Over dinner she excitedly related her findings.

196

# CHAPTER THIRTY-THREE

## — OF ALL THINGS, OR, WHO'D A THUNK IT? —

CLAIRE HAD DISCOVERED traces of very old kimberlitic pipes, several of them, but one was just 20 or 25 miles south of the village of Umiat. The pipe was tilted and worn and eroded, undiscovered until now, as it was masked by eons of gravel and rocky material slowly spreading north from the Brooks Range, by the many rivers flowing to the Arctic Ocean.

For hundreds of thousands, maybe millions of years, the Coleville River had been moving slowly east and then slowly west, crossing and then re-crossing the river delta along its way north to the Beaufort Sea. The signature of the kimberlitic calderas could be plainly seen in the Synthetic Aperture Radar returns, by anyone who knew what to look for.

So, maybe the miners from Circle City really had found diamonds in their sluice boxes. Diamonds could well be there or maybe in the mud of the Coleville River Delta and they might well be concentrated in several areas, one being a little south of the town of Umiat very near the Coleville.

Josh, hearing the news of the discovery, sat silently for a while, then simply said, "I'll drink to that." And he did.

The next weeks were filled with efforts to get the store in shape for winter as now snow was on the ground. There'd been a dusting the first week in September but it melted the next day. Jean and Skip went to Hawaii for two weeks and returned looking like they'd spent entirely too much time in the sun. Jean admitted they had gone to a nude beach to strut their stuff and she blushed as she told the story. Skip only smiled. They must've been in sipping cocktails the whole time too. Claire had never seen Skip so totally relaxed.

Matt Smith stopped by the store to deliver ten pounds of caribou sausage from Kevin and Molly, the friends in Bettles. Carter had recruited Matt for the flying job on the recommendation from Josh.

After one of his many trips back from the North Slope Matt stopped in at the Old Lodge in Bettles for a burger and soggy fries. He'd become friends with Kevin.

Kevin asked if Matt would take more Sausage to Josh and Claire at the store. He gave Matt a few pounds for himself as well. Kevin also told Matt about a recent plane crash just off the far end of the Bettles runway. It seems that the son of a mine operator, David Littlejohn, was killed in Super Cub in early September. He crashed as he was just leaving the runway: lost control on takeoff, must have stalled it out nearly 100 feet above the end of the runway. The plane had just been fueled up and it mostly burned on impact. Kevin was the first one to get to the site of the crash: he found part of the tail section of the plane that had not burned. He told Matt that one of the elevator control cables had parted; it seemed to have been badly corroded.

Lightning Source UK Ltd.
Milton Keynes UK
UKOW01n0308030318
318808UK00002B/2/P